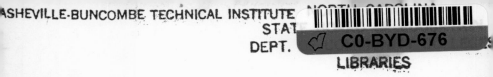

The Poison Summer

By Joe L. Hensley

THE POISON SUMMER
LEGISLATIVE BODY
DELIVER US TO EVIL
THE COLOR OF HATE

The Poison Summer

JOE L. HENSLEY

PUBLISHED FOR THE CRIME CLUB BY
DOUBLEDAY & COMPANY, INC.
GARDEN CITY, NEW YORK
1974

All of the characters in this book are fictitious, and any resemblance to actual persons, living or dead, is purely coincidental.

ISBN: 0-385-07474-3
Library of Congress Catalog Card Number 73–83638
Copyright © 1974 by Joe L. Hensley
All Rights Reserved
Printed in the United States of America
First Edition

The Poison Summer

Someone had dumped garbage on the walk that morning and used a wet piece of it to print crudely the word GET on the hood of my LTD.

My father's law office was on the second floor of a crumbling office building next to the Corbin County courthouse. I walked up those steps. Pop had "fallen" down them a few days back, but there was now nothing to show for it on the steps themselves. From the top I studied the steps some more. They were steep and Pop had complained about them on several occasions, but they seemed innocuous enough. I went on down the hall and used the key his secretary had grudgingly given me the day before at the cemetery. I was far ahead of that secretary, almost ahead of the morning sun. Sleep had been an elusive thing, easily frustrated by the first light of morning.

I sat in his swivel chair, feeling peculiar, knowing that here things, for a long time, had meant something to him.

From his window I could see the courthouse, all four floors of it. I could see the tower clock that tolled the hours. Already, in the very early morning, it was attended by its congregation of pigeons. In a way they reminded me of the curious and somehow hostile crowd that had, the day before, followed the hearse to the graveyard.

I got away from that.

By his desk was one of those rolling steel carriers, thick with the files of cases. There seemed to be a lot of files, although Pop had mentioned to me on my last visit that he was slowing down.

The case that had been most important to him, the one he'd called me about the night he'd died, was a murder first. That was the case which had brought the ghoulish horde of followers to the graveyard at yesterday's funeral. It probably was also the case that had caused the garbage to be dumped on Pop's walk. There'd been other incidents. Vandals had cut his office telephone line and broken into the office and slopped paint and offal on the walls and furniture. And there'd been calls and letters, a lot of them.

I'd read much in the newspapers about the murder. The governor of my state had told me even more about it, looking at it from a political viewpoint. He'd warned me not to get involved, and Pop, maybe sensing this, had not attempted to involve me and had tried it and lost it without my help. Once, before that trial, when we were fishing, I'd pried hard and gotten Pop to speak a few bitter comments about the case. That was the day he'd shown me the most recent of his threatening letters. He'd had half a lifetime of letters like that. A month later a jury had been out less than an hour and convicted Katherine "Kate" Powell.

I knew it was a warm case because of what I'd seen and heard when I'd come to visit my father. And, of course, I knew the woman, Kate Powell.

Dozens of reporters had covered the trial. It was, to the news media, a murder trial with about everything a newspaper in search of increased circulation dreamed of. There was a handsome, aging millionaire industrialist dead by poison in the midst of what news reports insisted on referring to as the tag end of a "wild party." There were lots of distinguished witnesses around to family and corporate disagreements. There was, most of all, Kate Powell. Her pictures in the news day after day had resurrected to life some of my old memories. There were accounts of public fights between Kate and Frank "Skid" Powell, and two juicy days of testimony about the supposed illicit romantic ventures of Kate.

I sat back in Pop's chair and remembered yesterday. The local paper had left me alone until after the services at the graveyard. But then they'd followed me back to Pop's house, hoping to milk one new headline out of me. A female reporter and a young boy photographer, with hair longer than hers.

I'd spread my hands. "I don't know anything about the Powell case," I'd said, without complete truth.

"Do you think there's any chance that your father's death might be connected with the case, Mr. Wright?"

I'd shook my head and smiled and played the careful buffoon for them, going into great detail about what I'd been doing in the capital at the very time Pop had fallen, going over again what the doctor had told me about Pop's fall, until she closed her notebook and he shuttered his camera, tired of my tedious conversation.

Anne Silver, Pop's secretary, had told me yesterday that Kate Powell was due for sentencing on the eleventh of July, three days away now. What the reporter and photographer really wanted to know was the part I'd play in the aftermath of the trial. Would I take the appeal? Would I replace my father?

Someone would have to take over. A conviction of murder means an almost automatic appeal. And Pop was dead.

He'd called me that last night and I remembered the

3

conversation. He'd said, after the amenities: "I'm onto something down here. Could you set it up so I could see the governor?"

"Maybe," I told him dubiously. "But he won't interfere. I know him well enough to be able to tell you that."

"I know him a little also," he said. "I'd like to see him."

"About the Powell thing?" I asked uncomfortably.

"Yes."

"Are you going to take an appeal?"

"You know I am. They jobbed me good, Mike."

"Then you ought to be able to get it reversed," I said.

"Will you help me get in to see the governor?" he asked again, his voice now not sure of me.

"I'll do what I can. When do you want to see him?"

"As soon as I can. It's getting a little tight down here. I think maybe they're watching me."

"Where are you now?" I asked.

"At the office. There was something I needed to look over again."

"Who's watching you?"

"I'll tell you about it tomorrow," he mumbled. "How about me coming up there?"

"Come ahead if you want."

"Can you fix it?"

"We'll talk about it," I said. Sometimes he drank too much and I wasn't sure this wasn't one of the times. He usually carried alcohol well and I couldn't tell now by his voice. But it was possible, maybe even probable.

It was after midnight when he'd called. Early next morning the building janitor had found him at the foot of the steps.

I sat at his desk and hand-riffled through the filing carrier and got out the file. The folder was depressingly massive. I opened it and looked at the covering sheets stapled to the front of the folder. One of the sheets had a list of witnesses who'd testified for the state. I was familiar with some of the prosecution names, G. P. Powell, Susan Powell, Charles Powell, Mayor Axe. Below that list was another, smaller one of witnesses who'd testified for the defense. With the exception of the name of Sheriff Ivan Alvie, I knew none of them.

There was a jury list also. One of those names I knew very well. It was circled on the list. He'd served as the foreman of the jury. Donald Kellogg. His name brought back my fourteenth summer, that short time of uneasy mother-father reconciliation.

That was the summer my mother and I had plotted and planned and escaped to come back to Lichmont, away from my grandmother and my Great-Aunt Hattie. I still believe that that pair were happy to see us go then and alarmed to see us return when things didn't work out. But even in their alarm there was a certain amount of satisfaction that their estimates of the possibilities of a reconciliation had been correct. The two of them had never trusted my father, or any other male. Great-Aunt Hattie's husband had run off to the Civil War in Spain and never returned, and my grandmother, despite bearing my mother, was a devout and practicing virgin from portal to portal who'd bullied her husband to an early grave. If there was any spark left in them for males, Franklin Delano Roosevelt and the great depression had put the last nail in their jointly held crucifix.

They'd hated and put on an iron-willed war against my boy child noise and clatter. Had it been possible I'm sure they'd have had me treated in the fashion of the several frustrated once male cats which softly peopled their house (held as joint tenants with a right of survivorship).

I knew that living with them all of those years had affected me. I'd never married. I'd gotten close once or twice, but it hadn't worked out.

They were both gone now—to a place where you can exist without love or hate, a place they'd practiced well for. They were never evil, but they'd only existed for all their days, carefully saving things for future time. And they'd assisted in the ruin of my mother's life. One time she'd broken away and married. Had she stayed with the bargain, maybe eventually she could have grown fond of it. But she'd run "home," unable to cope with Pop's temper and black moods, with his occasional drinking sprees. And so she'd set on the porch and rocked with them for the rest of her life. They'd even had the discourtesy to outlive her.

After that fourteenth summer I'd made my own way. I'd lived with Mother, but she'd blessedly managed to send me away to school. I hadn't seen much of Pop while I was growing up.

Closeness between Pop and me had come slowly, so that our last years, despite his more frequent spells of heavy drinking, had been better than our early years. He'd not been an easy man to know. I wasn't sure I was easy either. We'd come, a hundred and fifty years back, out of the deeps of the Welsh coal mines, and my father once passed on to me *the* family joke, without any humor in his eyes.

"Wrights," he said, "aren't happy above the ground and will even die to get back below it."

Sometimes I tried to imagine how it must have been between him and my mother. He, the dour, huge, bushy-browed male, unable to communicate anything when he was outside the courtrooms he loved, and she, near psychotic, needing to be treasured, made an idol of, shocked by the pain of my birth and that which went before and after.

6

They'd had a few chaotic early years plus that fourteenth summer year. Donald Kellogg, foreman of the jury, had been a part of my reconciliation summer. *Then,* he was a chunky boy with a nasty tongue and the bright white light of fourteen-year-old madness in his eyes. We'd fought and been good friends that summer, but it had been too many years. I'd seen him now and then in the years thereafter, but we'd never been "best" friends again.

The trial had lasted ten days, not overlong for a murder jury trial.

Pop had let me alone during the trial probably because I'd been out on exhibition to the politicians of my state. The governor was grooming me for further forays in the field. The politicians had done everything but check my back teeth and make me unzip.

The thing to do was believe implicitly that Pop had fallen down those damned steps. Anything else was insane. My difficulty was I wasn't sure, insane or not. Not really sure.

Inside the file there were scribbled notes on the trial itself. There was a sheaf of proposed instructions and the final instructions that Judge Stickney had read. There was a trial brief. I skimmed on down through the mass of papers to the last items in the file. Those were some good examples of various nasty letters that the representation of Kate Powell had brought Pop. Some of the letters were from religious nuts. Some were from other and assorted miscellaneous nuts.

Pop was dead.

The heat seemed to hang in a ball in the closed office.

I didn't really miss him yet. The vacant place inside was raw and I could skirt my way around it like a kid around the opening where a tooth had been removed.

It seemed to me that George Jett, chief of the Lichmont

Police Department, might do for a beginning point. I knew him a little. He'd be better than the sterile-appearing file to get an idea of what was going on now that the trial was done. It had been a while since I'd seen him. I had a perverse desire to pick him up again and look underneath and see whether he'd mellowed or soured. I knew he was a Powell man, but the town was Powell town.

Getting up was half the decision. Maybe I could just make a few cold noises and move on. Once, a long time back, I'd promised Pop that I'd fill in if he ever needed me, but I'd done it mainly because he'd been drinking when he asked. I could ease things along now, get out of it. Someone else could take the appeal. I nodded to myself, ready to be smart and political again.

I looked at my watch. It was still half an hour before the office would officially open. I looked around me. The office was three rooms. There was Pop's room, a secretary's room, plus a tiny library that opened out to an ancient fire escape. I walked on in there and tried the fire door, but it was locked or jammed and would not come open. I worked at it for a while and found what was causing the difficulty. Someone, probably the janitor, had jammed a nail under the door and pounded it in to hold the door tight. I took the nail out. It was bright and shiny although the door was rusted. I carried it back in and dropped it in the wastebasket.

I got my suit coat from an ancient coat rack. A picture of Abe Lincoln stared at me from the wall. Below the picture it read: "A lawyer's time and advice are his stock in trade." Yes, sir.

Outside, on the glass door, there was a sign. It read: "Wright and Wright." Down below it got specific: "Attorneys." It had been painted on that way right after I'd graduated from law school and Pop had never had it changed after I'd left the office.

With growing depression I felt a little more sense of loss as I admitted to myself that we would never try practicing law together again.

Outside, a group of early idlers were already lounging about the courthouse wall talking knife trades and dreaming dreams of wine by the barrel. Ragged farmers discussed the status of the crop year, their voices plaintive as they watched the sky and talked of needed rain. I reflected that individual life isn't long enough for most men to themselves accurately foretell the surge of the seasons. The measure of individual man is that he tries and believes that his desire can help bring the needed rain.

On a bench alone, in the middle of the courthouse yard, a big gaunt man sat watching me narrowly. His face was familiar and I knew him. His shirt was white with a high, old-fashioned collar and he wore a black string tie. He was very old and his face seemed like a bunch of marbles all laid out and ready for a game. He was holding a book with a cross on the front of it. The crowd of idlers seemed as aware of him as I was. They moved around him respectfully. He looked like some itinerant preacher come to save the town, but he wasn't a preacher. He was the circuit judge. Judge Stickney.

He nodded at me without a smile. "Come here, Mr. Wright," he ordered sternly.

I went up the steps and to his bench and he rose to meet me. He was a tall man used to command, but I was taller and I think he resented it.

"I'm sorry about your daddy," he said.

I shrugged. "The funeral was yesterday, Judge." He had not been there and both of us realized the insult of his failure to appear.

"The sentencing is Monday," he said. "I shall assume you'll be taking his place."

"Assume nothing, Judge Stickney," I said. "If I'm to appear you'll know it."

He smiled at me. "If you aren't there I'll appoint counsel for her. Makes no difference to me."

I nodded. "I'm sure it doesn't, Judge. My father told me about the trial. And I'll do about it what he'd have done about it."

His face went a little dark. "Your attitude is without promise, young man. Your manners are in need of mending. Perhaps, contempt . . ."

I smiled at him. "Are we in court out here, Judge?"

He had control back. "No, we aren't, Mr. Wright." He nodded at me and raised his voice for the crowd. "You be there for the sentencing, hear?" He looked away from me, sat down, and thumbed at his Bible. I'd been dismissed.

I stood for a second watching him. My father had hated the man but he had respected the office. I wondered what more the judge wanted from life before he left it. From what I knew the book with the cross on it hadn't taught him much.

I turned away. I nodded at the watchers along the sidewalk who furtively gave me looks of recognition, but life really didn't come back into the crowd until my wake calmed behind me. Lichmont was Powell town and I was opposing them because my father had opposed them. It wasn't safe or smart to be friendly to me.

Lichmont was also my native town, now grown to about sixteen thousand, county seat of a well-off farming area. I didn't really know the town well. I'd lived there for the first four years of my life, and then my parents had bitterly begun their first separation. Mother had taken me to her home, three hundred miles to the north and in another state, the place of the grandmother and the great-aunt, the place of freezing glances at boy noises, of rocking chairs constantly rocking on the porch—the fervent watching of life. My mother and my father had hated each other and loved each other for years by long-distance telephone and had reconciled only that once, the summer I was fourteen years old. It hadn't lasted. I'd come back to Lichmont intermittently while I was in college, after Mother died, moved on to the service, and come back again for a while after the service and after law school. I'd really never become a resident of Lichmont. We'd only tried each other out and not found a permanent fit. A part-timer, I knew, wasn't considered eligible for being raised to residency until he bought his cemetery lot and erected the stone and never received his final citizenship papers until the time he occupied his last Lichmont real estate under that stone. It was a town without much imagination, but it tried to make up for it with tradition.

It was also a town of much modest old money and one huge fortune—the Powell fortune. And the town revered that fortune.

The years away had not completely severed the umbilical cord between the town and me or my remembrance of "place" in the town. The Powells built the gymnasiums, endowed the chairs at the junior college, and added wings to the local hospital. My father had defended a woman who'd been accused and convicted of killing one of those Powells. The Powells ran their plant and made heavy news on the social pages of the Lichmont *Chronicle*. Thousands of people worked for them. They were the prime movers and shakers in Lichmont life. I had to remember that respectfully. They owned the town.

They also had political power.

Keep your head down, boy.

I remembered the town as a pleasant-appearing place. It had been a fair-sized town early, when my Welsh ancestors were already there, long before the first Powell had built a crude shed and begun making an alcoholic base patent medicine. The river had run through the valley from time immemorial, carving out the alluvial shelf and, an aeon before, helping raise in the ice age the hills that lay above the river. In 1840 the town had been populated by five thousand people. Now, most of the houses in the downtown area were old, remnants of that past time, built up to the edge of crumbling sidewalks on narrow lots. The business buildings were antique Federals and only God and the Chamber of Commerce helped the man who deviated from the design. The main street ran near the river and the big towboats moved sedately past during all four of the seasons of the town's year, snow, basketball, football, and golf, blowing their horns gently as they glimpsed each other. I had mostly loved the town, although it had never belonged to me. I had moved away from my father and secreted that love, but I knew it wasn't gone, merely dormant.

The town had not been, in its recent history, the most legal of towns. G. P. Powell and his administrators had the reputation of liking people to sip vigorously of the nectar of life. There were several bookie joints that I'd visited with and without Pop on occasion, and the main street always seemed to me to hold an excess of poolrooms and bars where summer-idled kids played neon pinball machines for open payoffs, while the older generation engaged in medium stakes poker in the back of the establishments. No one ever appeared to be upset about it and the games would always be politely closed while the yearly grand jury session was in progress. Minor sins. I remembered it had always been pretty much that way. The town gnawed at its sores only in and around election times. For the rest of it the streets seemed clean, the crime rate, as recorded at least, was low, the schools on a secondary level appeared adequate, and Pop had agreed once that the police were reasonably honest, never accepting the first offer.

Then there was Powell Junior College. It took up a part of the east end of the town and every year fielded a minor league football and basketball team and a token riot or two.

The Lichmont police had the entire basement floor of the new city building, only a few years old, cast in a ghastly Federal architecture imitation and in need of exterior painting. Some college vandal, rebel, or hippie (pick a current popular description) had painted an obscene word on the sidewalk in front of the building. Time and hard scrubbing had faded but not erased it. Without much imagination I could reconstruct the word even where it had faded worst. I said it salaciously aloud and looked up guiltily to see if I was observed.

Lichmont's fat little mayor stood at the swinging doors of City Hall and frowned at me and my dirty talk suspiciously. He'd added a mustache since the last time I'd seen him. His tie was askew and the bottom button on his shirt was either undone or missing. His eyes, in their web of fatty tissue, pondered and then placed me.

"Hello, Mayor," I said.

He nodded and gave me that innocuous grin that the Lichmont *Chronicle* likes to capture in their slightly yellow dog pages near election time. Albert Axe—Mayor Axe to me. Mayor and part-time Powell employee.

"Mike Wright," he said. "Too bad about your dad." He nodded at me, remembering. "You're up with the governor now, aren't you?"

"Yes."

13

He seemed a little nervous about that, but he swallowed and remembered bravely that it was his town. He brushed at the tattered mustache with one hand. Governors didn't pull much water down here on the river.

"What are you going to do on that Powell woman who poisoned her husband?" he asked, getting right to the point in a stage whisper. His look reminded me that we were all in this political business together. "I was a witness in the trial. You can tell me."

I leaned toward him conspiratorially. "I want to see the Chief on that. I wondered if maybe we couldn't work up a deal where he'd recommend a suspended sentence and a heavy fine." I winked.

He backed away a little. "No chance for her, laddie. None for you if you take a hand. And I wouldn't be flippant around this town about Powell affairs or police business."

"In that order?" I asked.

He shook his head and I waited for more, but he was cautious and done. He was going to fit me further in whatever niche I ground into before he said anything else showing where he was.

He said: "If there's anything we can do for you while you're visiting?"

"No," I said. "Not a thing."

A big car had stopped in front of the building. A horn blew once. The mayor gave me his grin again, its intent unknown.

"Got to go now. Ribbon-cutting time."

He waddled out to the car and I watched him fit himself inside. On the door of the car, an almost new Cadillac limousine, the words *Powell Chemicals Courtesy Car* were stenciled in old English script. The car sped away.

I found Chief George Jett in his office. He appeared unsurprised to see me and got up and shook my hand limply.

"How are you?" he asked. "We hear big things about you down here." He nodded at me with obscure satisfaction and dry-washed his hands. "I thought you might come in to see me. I heard around a few places that you were staying and were maybe going to take over your father's practice."

He waited for a reaction to that, but I gave him none. He wasn't a great deal older than I was. He was a thin man who took orders well. He was gangly and looked like a television good guy sheriff, but his eyes were as cold as a hillside creek when the snow first melts. When I'd started practice with Pop I'd gotten to know him. I knew he remembered that. We'd not liked each other then. I kept subpoenaing him into court and reminding him about what the constitution said and he kept ignoring me and the constitution and doing what he was told. He'd stayed and I'd gone.

"Sit down, please," he commanded.

I sat down on a hard chair.

"I thought maybe you'd talk with me about the Powell case," I said. "Then I wanted to ask you about Pop, too."

"The Powell case is done with," he said. "You'd be better off with a transcript of evidence."

"That won't be ready for a while. You're the chief of police and my records show you testified."

"That's right. But I testified for the prosecution."

I nodded and smiled at him disarmingly when his eyes met mine. "I know you don't have to talk to me now, but you're not employed by the state side of the case. It's done and surely you can talk about it. If I'm in it at all, I'm in late. What I'm trying to determine is what to do now that she's been convicted, I mean with Pop dead. I wasn't here for the trial and, like I said, it'll be a while for the tran-

15

script, at least until after the sentencing. But I'd like to find out some of what happened before the transcript is ready." I nodded. "You know, so I can determine what I need to do, make my decision."

He thought about it, and I thought, for a long moment, that he was going to refuse, but finally he nodded.

"Ask away," he said with a shrug. "Remember that what you ask isn't between the two of us. As a matter of course I'll tell G.P. and the prosecuting attorney all of what you asked and all of what I answered. But I talked to your daddy. I guess there's no reason not to talk to you. Not that what I say will do you a damned bit of good." His eyes came up to mine. "But first of all, what am I supposed to know about your father?"

"He died, Chief."

He nodded carefully. "I know that. He fell down some steps from what I heard." He looked away from me. "The janitor said he smelled like a gallon of booze. He drank some."

"Yes. I know. Did you check it out at all?"

"No reason," he said. "I did talk to the janitor."

"He got a lot of threatening mail."

He shrugged again. "So what? He was in an unpopular case, but it was over. *Why* would someone *wait* to hurt him?"

I said: "He didn't have a stroke. That isn't why he went down those steps. Doc Bush told me that."

"Okay," he said equably. "You show me something to interest me and maybe I'll get interested." He looked up at me. "You want to talk to me about the Powell case, then go ahead, but let's let your father rest in peace."

Almost I told him about the phone call, but caution prevailed. I decided against it. Even if I found something, I

16

wasn't sure I wanted him involved. And I didn't think the phone call would impress him much.

I said: "Why not start by giving me a little information about the Powell case in general? Do it as if I'd never heard of the case."

"Did you know Skid Powell when you lived here before?" he countered.

"A little. He was a lot older and out of my league. I knew who he was, of course, but I don't think I ever more than just met him. The only one in the family I personally knew is Charles. We went to law school together. They sent Charles to private schools before that. I guess Skid was his older brother."

"Half brother," he corrected. "How about the plant? Powell Chemicals?"

"I worked out there a summer when I was twenty years old. It's a big place. A lot of people worked there then. I guess a lot work there now. There weren't any unions then except a kind of a company union they slipped in to keep the other unions out."

He nodded. "Still that way. It's *the* local industry. And the Powells still don't like unions. I think they're right. They've never had a major strike out there. They keep six thousand people working at peak. Right now they're down from that a thousand or so and the town feels quite a pinch. But it's a good place to work." He nodded at me. "When someone named Powell got killed under suspicious circumstances we did all our homework. We put together a good case." He nodded again, eyes positive. "And we convicted her."

"Maybe you kind of had to convict her," I said softly.

His answer was quick. "A couple of my police commissioners are Powell people. Old man Powell likes to give pensioned policemen jobs and these are a couple of retired state police officers. Good men. Powell put the hammer on them and the mayor, but it was nothing illegal or even out of line. He just kept calling them, wanting to know what we were doing. Kept everyone moving on it more than anything else. He isn't real active at the plant these days and there was time for him to brood." He shuffled papers restlessly on his desk. "I'm sure you'll find he has a minor drinking problem. Skid's death hasn't improved it. Skid was the favorite son. So I got pressured and the prosecutor got pressured—Jim True's prosecutor. But all we were ever asked for was action. He got that right quickly. It wasn't too tough a case."

"I see. Did the rest of the family join with him?"

He shook his head. "Not really. He's the head man. There's a daughter who was some years younger than Skid. She has her father's views, but she isn't quite as forceful about it. She has problems of her own, I guess. She's married to Dave Jordan. He runs the plant now when the old man will let him. That's how Skid ran it, too, with the old man peekin' over his shoulder. Then there's the old man's wife—I guess she's maybe his third or fourth. Miss Susan. She's a woman who used to work out at the plant and then at the courthouse before he married her. And of course there's Charles, the one you know. He gave your daddy some trial help and there's hell to pay over that." He smiled and it wasn't a completely pleasant smile.

"What's the old man's given name?"

He looked slightly surprised. "Those that know him pretty well call him G.P. I don't know what the initials stand for. I usually call him Mr. Powell."

"I've been considering asking for a continuance of the sentencing date," I mused, to sort of try it out.

"Oh?"

"Yes. Let her get someone else. It really isn't my kind

of case. Too late now. I don't know much about it. It ought to be appealed by a lawyer who specializes in murder cases, one who does a lot of appellate work."

For the first time he lost a part of the faint, bored expression he'd had since the telling of the Skid Powell story began. "Up to you," he said slowly. "If you're going to ask for any more time then I'd better stop talking to you right now. If I don't then sure as hell the word would get back to the mayor and the Powells that I talked to you and maybe said something that helped cause the delay." He nodded. "I might wind up without a stripe." He grinned. "Four years to go."

"Is it that bad?" I asked.

He looked at me. "Three city councilmen are Powell employees. The others have Powell people in their families. They encourage politics out there. And Mr. Powell wants things to move!"

"Isn't anyone on Skid's wife's side around this town?"

He dry-washed his hands solemnly again and I decided it must be a nervous gesture.

"She's got them on her side up at the jail," he said softly. "The sheriff's some kind of relation to her. He was a witness for her at her bond hearing and at the trial. She didn't get bond and she was convicted, but he lets her have pretty much the run of the jail." There was minor outrage on his face. "How about that? Denied bail, convicted of capital offense, yet she still runs the radio for the county sheriff. And the word on that is around and some of the citizenry like to poke fun with it at my boys. You wait until he runs again. He'll get stomped."

"Will he now?"

"Sure. I mean he's made a regular trusty out of her. Sits her right up there in the office as bold as brass communicating with my people, talking with them on the radio. And we arrested her."

"Maybe he knows something you don't."

He laughed without humor. "In this town? Sheriff and the Powells had it hot last election. Powells tried to beat him and didn't get the job done. They will next time. You don't beat Powells twice. Your daddy didn't have no illusions about it." He nodded. "Like I said, we talked about the case some. Your dad had common sense," he finished, doubting mine with a look.

"Tell me about that."

"He said it was the kind of thing that jury either believes or fails to believe. In this town people either love the Powells or hate them. Kate Powell said she didn't, a lot said she did, so they juried it." He grinned. "He thought maybe the jury would hang up and he could maybe make a bond for her after that. So he toned her down some when they got her in jail. He put her in long dresses for the trial. Used to be, before she went to jail, that her skirts were so short you could get your hopes up high every time she sat down or got up. Skid bought those mini skirts for her and made her wear them. Then he'd get mad when other men looked. And I guess they did look. The testimony showed how she was slipping around with a very sharp captain who used to be a part of the officer cadre out at the plant. A Captain Joe Ringer. He's dead now too. Got killed across the water shortly after Skid died. Right after he got to Asia. Ringer was at the party that night. Him and Colonel Harrigan. We questioned Ringer before he was transferred, but he wouldn't own up to going with her or admit slipping her any strychnine that he'd maybe borrowed out at the plant." He waved a negligent hand. "I questioned him myself. There never was anything to hold him on. I don't think any of the Powells tried to keep him from being transferred."

"Where'd she get the poison?"

"You can get strychnine lots of places. Animal poison. She could have gotten it at the plant." He stopped, at a loss for a moment, then remembered his thread. "Your dad was trying to clean her up, maybe make someone on the jury believe in her, someone he could get on it who hated the Powells." He shook his head. "But it didn't work that way." He looked away and then back. "You can get ten to one around here in the books that she'll get the death penalty when they sentence her Monday. The old man wants it. That's always been enough for almost everyone around here." He nodded stoutly at me. "You wait and see. The judge'll do what he ought to do."

"What do you think that will be?"

He answered carefully with an answer I thought he'd formed long before. "In my opinion she was guilty. I testified to facts. I think she'll get the chair. And she'll burn if the Supreme Court allows it. Be glad I'm not judge." He shook his head. "They tried her first class, Mr. Wright. She was a lot of woman, but when they got at it they hammered her down to size. She's from out in the Walnut Hills part of town. You remember where that is? It's as close as we get around here to ghetto. Mixed black and white and brown, all poor. There are a lot of houses out there that are bad enough to cause a congressional investigation, if the right people complained. Last year there were a couple of verified starvation deaths out there. God knows how many there actually were that weren't even suspected. Kate Powell's mother was at least part Mexican. She died when Kate was about three. Her daddy was one of the town drunks thereafter. There was a small scandal when her mother and father got married. He was from a fair family and she was a pretty little nothing. He died a few years back. The book upstairs in the city court office will show he was a frequent visitor. Drunk all of the time. Gave up when his woman died. No one in this town could believe that Kate could grow up out there untouched by it all. No way. She was in trouble when the trial began, just from what the town thought."

"How'd she meet Skid?"

"Way I heard it she was working for a jeweler downtown. She'd been married before—her first man was killed in some kind of industrial accident—out at the plant." He looked at me. "Maybe you knew him. Alvin Tucker. One of the Tuckers used to live out in the Midwood area east of town. I guess he'd be about your age or a little older if he'd lived."

I shook my head. The name meant nothing.

"Anyway, she took the workmen's compensation settlement from the insurance company and used it for some business schooling and clothes and then she went to work. Skid saw her and gave chase. He was like a bull in early spring. She held out for marriage. Skid had never been married before. He was about fifty and she was maybe in her late twenties and him with a bad case of the red pepper hots." He grinned to himself, the perennial police philosopher, repeating once again the often told barracks tale: "I thought he'd be dead in a couple of years maybe— of natural causes. Maybe she did too. He fooled the lot of us. Powells are tough people. They even acted happy together for a bit. Of course the family screamed when Skid married her. There was talk around town, too. I know her blood's part Spanish or Mex, but a lot of people like to say it's a touch of tar." He looked up at me quickly. "You know how it can be?" He fell into silence, maybe remembering it.

"I know," I prompted.

He came back to me. His own narration had gotten to him and there was a bit of animation on his narrow face now. "In the year before Skid died she sued him for divorce a couple of times and he sued her a couple. There was a divorce pending when Skid died, but they'd made it up and it just hadn't been formally dismissed yet. Your dad didn't represent her in the divorce actions. She always went out of town for lawyers to get them filed. Maybe she had to. Anyway, they'd reconciled at a picnic that afternoon and they were having a little party out at the house that night to celebrate. Witnesses heard them argue and her threaten to kill him. Then things kind of smoothed out a little. They were still mad, but they quit arguing. There were some witnesses who testified that a little later she served him his last drink. Then Doc Bush and some state toxicologists testified he died from strychnine poisoning and estimated the poison had to have been given to him within a short time of when he died. It isn't a very good way for a man to die. Somehow the glass he drank out of got picked up and disposed of before we got there, and your dad jumped on that, but it didn't help him much that I saw." He nodded to himself. "Talk to Doc Bush. He's the coroner."

"Strychnine," I mused.

He nodded. "A very nasty poison. It's deadly enough to kill quickly, easily available and, like I said, a bad, bad way to die. There are some pictures taken after he was dead. Judge Stickney let them in and the jury saw them."

"I'll bet he did," I said. "How about the accused? Was she drinking also?"

"Sure. It was one of their usual parties. The contest in the whole crowd seems to be who can get bombed fastest." He grimaced. "Turn the lights down a little, wait late, and chase after each other when you get enough liquor to raise the courage. It was out at the 'Acres.' That's what Skid called his little shack. Couple of hundred thousand dollars' worth of brick and thermo-pane with an indoor swimming pool and a full four-car garage. There were maybe twenty-thirty people around during the course of the evening, but most had left. The old man, G.P., kept staying and I guess him being there and then the argument put a damper on things. Check your father's file. Some of those people saw Skid die. The Mayor, for one. Some testified that they saw Kate Powell deliver him drinks throughout the course of the evening. G.P. and Geneva saw her put something in his last drink." He spread his hand. "It wasn't a tough case."

"Maybe if there was pressure put on you and the prosecutor—then some of those witnesses got a little pressure, too."

"That's legal figuring," he said. "And it can only get you in trouble around this office."

I refused to get ruffled, sensing he might want me to do just that.

"Where'd she get the poison?" I asked again, curiously.

He looked away. "It was never shown. It's easy to get. Like I said, maybe it came from the plant, from her fancy soldier."

"Mrs. Powell would be a little over thirty now?" I asked. I knew the answer, but I wanted him to keep talking.

He figured by looking away from me again. "I suppose so. She's a most attractive woman. The town had a lot of talk going about her and Skid and some of those parties. They tell it that sometimes Skid would drink too much and pass out and Johnathon would wind up taking him home. She'd come later, when everything was done." He grinned suggestively.

"Who's Johnathon?"

"I guess the best way to describe him would be to call him Skid's companion. A butler, handy man, friend. He worked for Skid before and after the marriage. Johnathon Hartwick. He wasn't around for the trial. Your dad got some use out of that. Johnathon was making the drinks in the kitchen for a while, but not for the last hour or so. Testimony showed he was passed out in his bedroom. So he didn't do your dad much good. Anyhow, they convicted her."

"Tell me about these other men and Mrs. Powell?"

"There was considerable testimony about that. I heard that most of it concerned this Captain Ringer. I'll bet Skid didn't know. He'd have tried kicking the hell out of anyone he caught fixing to fool with her. I know that. That soldier boy was twenty years younger than him, but I'll bet old Skid would've tried him." He smiled to himself, remembering again. "Skid was a peculiar article. Right before he died he bought himself one of those wigs they make for men these days. It was long and blond and cut modern. He had a fifty-year-old face that looked like someone had mowed grass to shape it, all deep wrinkled by the sun. His main feature was a nose with a hundred thousand miles of bourbon on it since his last oil change. When he put on that wig and smiled I'll bet he looked like the mother of Mona Lisa."

"How about lie detector tests?"

He nodded. "We gave them out in batches. Johnathon took one and so did Kate, I think she even took it twice. Inconclusive on her and the state man said Johnathon was telling the truth."

"That's a convenient result," I said.

He flushed. "You sound like some of the out-of-town newspapers. So she's pretty? So she says she didn't do it?

So when she was convicted the old man paid the reward money into the police benevolent fund? All that doesn't mean we didn't do our job."

"There was a reward?"

He nodded. His telephone rang and he answered it and I sat there politely and waited, not really sure I wanted to ask him any more for now. I had the story and it seemed a simple enough case. They had her now. I wondered how much of their having her had been caused by the pressure that the old man, G. P. Powell, had exerted, his money, his reward?

Chief Jett hung the phone up and looked at me inquiringly, waiting.

"Thanks for talking to me," I said.

"Are you going to stay here?" he asked quickly, wanting to feel me out, wanting to sort out whatever possible power struggle might be coming. He had four years to go.

"Way I heard it," he said, without waiting for my answer, "is that you're some kind of wheel up there in the Statehouse. I even heard you might be on the ticket next time for one of those big offices." He stopped, intent on me.

"Never believe political talk," I said.

"Don't cause no trouble," he warned me carefully when I left.

I went out of the air conditioning and into the stifling heat. A haze of smog now covered the town. Some of the smell was medicinal. Powell Chemicals.

I walked on up to the corner. In front of the Moose Club there was an empty bench. I sat down and watched City Hall. People came and went in a leisurely manner. In a bit Chief Jett came out, talked in what seemed to me to be an idle fashion to a big, cow-faced, uniformed patrolman, then left driving a black Dodge with a buggy-whip antenna. I wondered where he was going.

I sat there on the bench and remembered what had happened with the governor.

Four days back at this time of the day I'd been on the top floor of the Statehouse admiring the State Supreme Court chambers and talking to one of the judges I knew casually.

While I was doing that my father was dying.

When I tired of talking, I walked back downstairs to the office and to the cubbyhole that had been partitioned off for me. For a time I sat there figuratively twiddling my thumbs, watching the telephone, wanting it to ring and for the call to mean something, but it didn't ring. I admitted to myself that I was more than bored. I admitted it for perhaps the five hundredth time. And I wondered how long Mike Wright could sit and twiddle without losing that something inside that keeps one from being ill at ease when his own reflection is seen in a mirror. I was better at construction than maintenance.

The magnificent Sarah, who was *his* personal secretary and who all of us around the governor agreed we were in love with, came into my hole and said: "He wants to see you, Mike."

"*He*," of course, was the governor. Foster Huffman.

I followed tamely behind her. She was pushing fifty, but she still had a nice walk and the girdle kept things from wobbling. And she was still interested that other people were interested.

In my state the governor inhabits an office about the size of a large barn. Squarely in the middle of his huge office there's a desk that looks like it came out of Hollywood. It's big and ornate and it's surrounded by couches and chairs, room for maybe a hundred to sit. The room

27

had never been real to me. It seemed to me that the room had surely been intended for a dance floor or a gymnasium and some early, arrogant governor had commandeered it.

In one of the tiny anterooms I waited out a couple of visiting dignitaries who were having their pictures taken with the *man*. He saw me at the door and nodded at me, his eyes serious. Then he set his face into the well-known, smiling public mask just before the flash bulb went off. When the visitors were ushered out I went in.

I'd known Governor Foster Huffman for a fair amount of time. I'd been a part of his law firm for two years after I left Pop and before Huffman had gotten the bug to run for governor. I'd helped when it hadn't seemed possible before the state convention, then represented him on the state committee after the convention and after his nomination when it became possible.

We were friends. I liked him. He owned a keen, incisive mind and a brilliant ability for detail. I thought he'd made a fair governor so far, although I doubted he'd really be credited with being one. Credit goes, these days, only to the governor who gives more service than all predecessors, fights the questing hands of subordinates away from the public till, makes no one mad except the student groups, who are always angry anyway and so don't count, and lowers (or at the very least doesn't raise) taxes.

He motioned me down to a chair. The sun from his window shown on his graying hair. I reflected that he was twenty years older than I, but it had never seemed so. He was born to be a corporate lawyer. In the campaign he'd been devious, demanding, cunning, and at times politically naïve. He wasn't naïve any longer.

"Your father's had some kind of an injury," he said seriously and unexpectedly. "We got the call only a few minutes ago. Sarah talked with the doctor." He held up a soothing hand. His voice was low and hypnotic. "The report is that he seems to be doing all right. He fell down some steps. He's unconscious and the doctor said he'd undoubtedly stay that way for a while. They're trying to determine his injuries." He folded his hands. "You'll want to go down?"

"Of course," I said. "Right now."

He nodded. "And you'll want to stay a while."

"Yes," I said, sensing something in his voice, an undertone of disapproval.

"I want you back as soon as possible. Don't get involved in local problems." He gave me his piercing look. "I need you here, you know."

I smiled at him a little, remembering my morning. "For what?"

He spread his hands. "I know it isn't much of a job, but it gives you exposure."

He was right about that and so I nodded.

"I hope you'll stick it out."

I waited, knowing there was more.

He smiled and looked a little away from me, seeing the future. "You've got it in your blood and you have the touch. I see you walk into a room and you fill it. They all know you're there. You're not pretty, but you're big and you've got something, call it charisma. You could go all the way." He eyed me. "And don't say you aren't interested."

"I'm interested."

"Your father made his own mess down there," he said.

"How's that? What do you mean by 'mess'?"

He shrugged and refused my questions with one of his own: "How come you didn't stay in practice with him?"

I shook my head. "No good reason. A multitude of small things. I wanted to make my own decisions. His practice wasn't very busy and it wasn't very interesting. And I kept trying to do things the way the Constitution says you can do them and not getting very far down there. That was when Judge Morgan was on the bench. He died a year or two back and there's a new judge I don't know very well. Governor Kerrigan appointed him—Judge Stickney. He couldn't be much worse."

"Powell family runs Lichmont," he said. "A fellow in your shoes should be careful of them."

"I know that. Big money."

He leaned back in his massive chair. "We got substantial help out of them in the campaign. They are heavy contributors to the party. Your dad was on the other side of them defending a woman who poisoned one of the sons."

"I've read about it and Pop's talked about it, Governor, but it's over. She was convicted."

He snorted. "Down there, with them on the other side, it won't be over until the last page has been turned. It might be a lot better for you to let someone else take over for her if your father can't continue. There are lots of lawyers, but only one governor at a time." He watched me carefully, having gotten out what he wanted now and having managed to ignore my comments on it.

"I'm to stay out of it, then?" I asked stiffly.

"You have to go through a few conventions before you can wind up sitting where I'm sitting. Lots of money can change things. The Powell family has lots of money." He looked away from me, seemingly not satisfied with what he was seeing. "Do what you want."

"I made a deal with Pop when I left that if anything went wrong and he really needed me I'd come back and help," I said. "I thought he might ask me to help him in the trial, but he didn't."

He turned slightly away. "You don't really have to help him now."

30

I nodded. "You're right. I don't have to. I'll see how it goes. Maybe the woman . . ."

He brought his eyes back to me, appraising me, digging into me with his intuition. "You know the woman, don't you? The one who was convicted?"

"Yes," I said, looking back into the dimness of time, down all the lost years. "I know her."

After a while I got tired of sitting and figured nothing was going to take place at the police station and that Chief Jett wasn't going to come back in the firm, entangling grasp of the Powells. It wouldn't be like that. Nothing hard line, nothing definite. Just a chain of command starting at G. P. Powell and moving on down through the mayor and the City Council. . . .

I walked on up a side street. The jail was four blocks away and so I stayed on the side street, avoiding the main street merchants' prying eyes. The side street had shade trees and sparse traffic. The trees had grown tall and the leafy shade and the smell of summer leaves was good. As I walked I could see down between houses all the way to the river. It was at pool stage and the ground along the edges seemed baked and hard.

I cut up through an alley to the jail. The jail building was painted a neat white and it looked like something left over from an old Civil War movie. It squatted in the middle of its square block with a park on one side and asphalt parking area on the other. A sign on the door invited me to *walk in* and so I did.

I didn't really know Ivan Alvie, the sheriff, very well. I'd known him vaguely when he'd been chief deputy, just about well enough then to nod to. Now he was sheriff. He sat behind his paper-heaped desk and nodded at me while a deputy lied gallantly on the phone telling someone that

Alvie was absent. The sheriff turned away from me momentarily and surveyed the wavy reflection of his fat, old form in the window behind.

I knew some things about him. He'd worked his way into the office by outliving the previous sheriff and being slightly less unpalatable than the rest of the candidates. I decided that if he was allowing Kate Powell special treatment and privileges there had to be more than political reasons for it. Being friendly with her didn't appear to be smart in Lichmont.

We weren't members of the same political party and being sheriff is about as political an office as a man can have. Anyone can run for it and, year after year, many do. I remembered my father had written to me that Alvie had defeated a round dozen competitors in his party's primary. My not being of his party might or might not be a disadvantage. If he was pushing for Kate Powell, I figured he would probably treat me as an ally.

He smiled at me and added and subtracted things about his world and mine in his eyes and I was the winner by it. His voice was high and thin and startling in so gross a man. His hands trembled as he lifted them nervously. There was an odor about him, an effluvium, that I'd smelled before. I thought it might be the smell of a heavy drinker. His eyebrows were shaggy and needed trimming and there was a recurrent tic near his right eye.

"Yo there, young Mr. Wright," he said. "Miss Kate and I were awful sorry about your dad. Even if he lost her case we know he did the best he could for her and he was a fine man. I had to work the traffic on the funeral." He nodded. "One of the biggest funerals I ever saw here. A lot of the town liked your dad."

"As many as like the Powells, Sheriff?"

He assayed me with a penetrating glance. "I'd say so. He

gets his way most times, old G.P. does. Now someone's going to have to take over and try to help Miss Kate against him. I guess you'd do that? You'd be the natural one."

I shook my head. "I don't know. I shouldn't. I need to get back upstate as soon as I can." The lie, glibly told, made me look away from him and I said compromisingly to the wall: "Maybe I could talk to her and discuss it and we could decide what to do—what she needs. She really ought to have someone who specializes in criminal law, someone to do the appeal work."

"Your dad thought that if he could find something, some bit of new evidence, that maybe he could convince Judge Stickney to grant us a new trial, but I doubt it. Not Judge Stickney. He's all paid for by the Powells. But your dad thought he might." He nodded at me. "You can hear a lot of nasty things around town, about the jury and the pressure some of them got. You hear things about the judge, too."

"Like what?"

"A lot. Like Stickney takes orders from G.P. Like a couple of men on the jury who worked at the plant got layoff notices right before the trial began. They didn't get called back until the trial was over. A couple of others live in houses owned by Powell Realty and houses are hard to find around here. Like anonymous phone calls to some of the others, the ones who could be calculated to be impressed with phone calls. The caller would say that Kate ought to be found guilty and anyone who didn't find her guilty was as bad as Kate was—that sort of thing. Old G.P. was making sure."

"Why'd Pop try it here? Why didn't he venue it somewhere else? At least have a special judge?"

"Your dad thought it was as good here with Stickney as anywhere else. He was wrong, but we all agreed. A few

33

people around town are mad at all the high pressure. They don't talk heavy, though. Not with G.P. in the picture."

"If you could get affidavits from jury members you could probably use them to help."

He shook his head. "I can find out a little about what happened, but no one here wants to bell the cat. It's hard to get anyone to sign anything." He scratched himself vigorously. "I've tried." He grinned without humor. "You may find it that way too."

"I've been involved in some appeals. Most of them go pretty straight down the line in upholding a verdict."

"Well, there's the governor," he said suggestively.

I shook my head. "I think I'm on my own in this."

He nodded, but without conviction.

"Chief Jett seems to believe she got convicted rightly and that it's all over now," I said, to test his reaction.

He sniffed audibly. "Jett's like ninety-five per cent of this town. Someone says G. P. Powell to them and they bow down and kiss what's handiest." He stopped and looked away. "Maybe it's all done. I had my hopes pinned on that jury. Even if they thought Kate killed him, God knows they had plenty of reason to know old Skid needed killing. He needed it almost as bad as that drunken daddy of his. A real pair to draw to: Both of them circular never-ending sons of bitches with paid-up dues cards."

"Tell me about them," I said.

He shook his head. "What for? Kate can tell you ten times more about them than I can. And maybe I'm just wasting my time in the telling." He looked at me, almost angry now. "She needs you, Mr. Wright. I need you to help her. Her father and my wife were blood cousins." Something old and half forgotten smoldered in the back of his eyes. "None of my wife's people were much pleased when he married that Mex woman, but that time is a generation

34

past now. I stick by my blood and my wife's blood. And Kate testified she didn't kill that no good bastard." He nodded coldly. "All the case they had, you're going to find if you try to help, is what the Powells put up against her. What they bought and pressured. I suppose it'll be enough. But she's got to have a lawyer if only for the formalities." He looked away from me and his voice decreased in volume. "I had the whole bunch against me last election. They nominated one of their own on the other ticket. I mean all of them—Skid, Charles, G.P. worked against me. They even had that one that looks like he was strained through a sheet out working—the one that married the Powell girl. They fought me mean and they fought me dirty. They passed out hate sheets about me at their plant out there. They bought votes. But I won me the election. I'd trade it for Kate now. I'm going to continue to believe in her. No matter what a bought jury said different." He lowered his voice even more, as if afraid that someone might hear. "They maybe set her up for it, Mr. Wright. I just don't know the how or why."

I almost turned away. I had heard that song before, but I wanted to see her again. "Can I talk to her?" I asked.

"Sure you can," he said, his voice more hearty. He turned away and I thought I saw a tiny smile. "You want I should get her now?"

"If you would."

He nodded and extricated a huge metal key from a drawer. He motioned me to wait.

"I lock her in the women's quarters at night. Saves talk," he said apologetically. "And me an old man."

He left me and I sat in his office and slapped at flies while the air conditioner chugged futilely in the window. I read the closest wanted poster on the nearby wall with-

35

out real interest. It described someone wanted for revolutionary acts. The description, I decided, might fit me.

The girl who followed the sheriff back into the room seemed too slender, but she was the girl I remembered.

I sat in my chair not knowing whether I could breathe and I watched her. The deputy had vanished and there were only the sheriff and the girl and me.

I wondered if she remembered me.

Sheriff Alvie sat behind his desk and looked us over curiously. I believed he was trying to read my reaction to the girl and I tried hard to keep it unapparent and didn't feel completely successful.

She was over thirty years old now, about my age. The only place I could read that quantity of age was in her amber eyes. Somehow they were very old eyes, but they were, at the same time, innocent eyes. Their look of innocence meant nothing, I knew. I have known women with knowing, dirty eyes whom I found to be prim and virginal. I have known other women with innocent eyes who'd never really known the meaning or power of the word from the time of their twelfth birthday.

Her legs were trim and very good and the body they supported was curved and coltish, a young girl's body, never used hard for childbirth, if I was any judge.

There were no lines in her face and her complexion was dark, but seemed flawless. The face was more elegant than beautiful, but there was a sort of beauty there, so that repeated inspections each brought the impact of something new. As she turned the face it seemed to me that each new outline that I saw was somehow better than the previous ones. It was, over all, a finely drawn face, showing magnificent bones behind flesh that seemed near transparent.

Her hands were slim and she held them rigidly at her sides, under control, with only a slight tremor. As I watched she brought one hand up hesitantly and ran it through hair that was of such a shade of brown that it almost had rust reflections, very deep and full of life. It cascaded down behind her and was caught and held in a loose ribbon.

She was a tall woman and she had a look of command. The gaunt look and the harried lines around her eyes were the only upsetting things about her. I thought her to be the type of woman who is born to be the envy and despair of all other women—the kind who can run negligent hands through her hair and comes out looking better than the normal woman after two hours under a dryer—the kind who can put on a bargain basement dress and look more attractive than other women in their best frocks—the kind of woman who looks young to fifty and mysterious for the rest of her time and fills a church with mourners, all wondering why the others are there.

Looking at her, I made a second guess about the trial. I wondered if my father had been careful about seating women on the jury who were of an age with her and therefore in competition with her. There'd surely have been an instinctive desire to want to punish that face and body from a competitor woman, maybe without even knowing why. And Pop might have been to the age where such could be unapparent to him. Too late now, of course.

The sheriff said: "This here's Mike Wright. He's the son. I suspect you and him ought to be talking together, Katie."

I nodded at her and moved a little, feeling as if I'd turned all elbows.

She examined me with curious amber eyes. "Are you going to take your father's place and be my lawyer for what's left of it?" she asked.

"I don't know," I said hesitantly.

"Your father talked about you. He told me he didn't

know you as well as he wanted. You went away with your mother and he didn't see much of you when you were growing up." She nodded at me, seemingly remembering more. "He told me once he might call you to come down and help him with the trial. But he didn't do that." She stopped for a moment and fixed me in the sights of her eyes. "He didn't call you, did he?"

"No," I said. "But he talked about you a little and I asked him some things about the case." I stopped and waited. Her voice was very dark and good. Being near her was like being iron near a magnet.

"I didn't kill him, Mr. Wright," she said very softly, and I leaned as close as I dared. "I swear it."

"Yes. All right."

"We were at our place. He fell over. He was gasping and trying for breath and I thought he'd had another heart attack." She shook her head and took her eyes away from me. "He said I'd killed him. They let people testify to that. Then G.P. tried to beat me with his cane. Miss Susan stopped that. She's his wife and the only one who's really nice. There was a time before the doctor came."

"Do you know what strychnine is?"

She nodded. "Where I grew up we all knew about strychnine—there were rats. And I know it's the poison the newspapers say killed him."

"And did you serve him his drinks?"

"Yes. At least some of them. He always drank bourbon and cola. I've tried to bring that evening back into focus, but it all seems blurry now. John was making drinks for a while in the kitchen and I helped some there."

"Johnathon Hartwick?"

"Johnathon Hartwick," she said, agreeing, "I got one there for Skid maybe an hour before he died. John had gone to his room by then. I don't think I got him any others after that. Skid must have been on another drink when he . . ." She shook her head and looked away and then came back to me with her haunted eyes. "They said I gave him his drinks. I'm afraid I didn't help myself much. I just wasn't sure that I hadn't. And there were all those witnesses, even the mayor. Most of them worked for the Powells out at the plant, but they were the ones who were at the party—there weren't other witnesses." She shook her head again. "But, as God is my judge, I didn't kill him. I swear it to you." She looked away from me and I saw her lose something of herself in realization. "But I swore it to them, didn't I? And it didn't do me any good. Why should you believe me when they didn't believe me?" She smiled at me, a sad smile. "It's all done and over with, isn't it?"

"Maybe," I said. "Maybe not."

"I feel sure it is."

"Tell me more about it," I coaxed. "You said he was drinking?"

She nodded. "A drink didn't last him long, Mr. Wright."

"Mike," I said. "When you call me Mr. Wright I still look behind me for my father."

"I was so terribly sorry about him," she said. "I thought maybe there were some times during the trial that he didn't seem well. It seemed like he'd be all right in the mornings and in the afternoons he'd just sort of wear out."

I nodded. If I discounted the possibility that Pop might have been pushed down his office stairs, then it got down to how badly I wanted to be in this. It wasn't exactly biting at the hand that fed, but it certainly wasn't licking it, either. It was politically stupid to go further and all I had to do was bow and mutter politely and move away. She was a lovely woman who'd been convicted of killing her husband and we were into the last act on that. I'd met her what seemed a hundred years before and she had been my first love. So what?

I remembered that dreary little hole of a room adjacent to the governor's office and the phone that rang now and then. I thought about the too many people who knew you could buy it all with a word to the right man and maybe you could at that. People like the Powells, people with money and/or power. I thought about the many and tiresome mornings after, when the medicinal double martinis of the night before had faded to green dust and all that stretched before me was the ache of another dreary day in that room.

Too many things were in my way. Mostly she was in my way. Being close to her made me reckless, defiant. Maybe I could get away with it. Maybe I could convince the governor that it was a thing of honor. He was a great one for honor. Besides, a few days wouldn't hurt much.

It felt good to tentatively decide for it. Good—and sort of stupid.

"We did have fights," she said. "We fought most of the time. We had a dilly that night."

"Did you say to him that you were going to kill him?"

She nodded. Her eyes were abject. "It was an expression we both used too much. I used it that night. Others heard it and testified about my saying it." She nodded again, this time to herself. "Bad luck for me, I guess. I tried to call it off. I mean the marriage. I told him I didn't want his money. I just wanted him to leave me alone. But he wouldn't do that." She looked up at me. "I left him a lot of times, but he'd find me and force me to come home."

I raised my eyebrows. "How?"

"Any way he could. He'd break in where I was if he had to—use physical force to make me come back. He'd hire people to follow me around when he went on trips. Sometimes I think he paid them extra so that they'd try to get me to go out with them. And after he was gone I was sorry, maybe even lonely." She sighed and shook her head in exasperation at her own complex emotions, unable to understand them. Her eyes went bleak. "Do you think there'd be any chance that they'd help me if I turned the house over to them, signed over any interest I had in his stock in the company, gave it all to G.P.? Maybe that would be best." She shivered. "I've got to be free, outside. I think of having to go to another place where the cage is tighter and something inside me just shrivels away."

"Did he make a will?"

"There was one. Your dad showed me a probated copy. Half to me, the other half split between G.P. and Geneva, share and share alike. The bank is the executor. I know they transferred the shares to G.P. and Geneva. Your dad said the will wasn't any good as to me if I was convicted."

I nodded. That was right. "Was the house in both of your names?"

"Yes. He changed it that way right after we were married. I saw the deed. It had his name and my name and then 'husband and wife.'"

I nodded, thinking. The house then came to her by operation of law—at least I thought it did.

"Did you get some offer on the property and stock?" I asked.

She hesitated. "I suppose I really didn't, but they're fighting again about who runs the plant. They've fought about it for years—always fighting—each other, anyone. I got tired of the fighting. Skid never seemed to. And there's the stock willed to me. Maybe it could make a big difference in this fight."

"Then there's a stock fight going on?"

She nodded, not really sure. "I think so."

"If there is a real fight about it I'd like to know about it," I said to her, and then looked meaningfully over toward the sheriff.

He shook his head, not knowing either. "All I know is that G.P. took a restraining order. Had it brought over here for me to read to her. Before that they sent a man in here and wanted her to sign a proxy—I think for the old man—G.P. When she wouldn't sign, then they got the order, but I heard they were going to get one anyway, in case she changed her proxy. Under the order she can't do anything with the shares."

"Have you got a copy of the order that was served?"

He nodded and went over to dig through his files. I watched.

Her voice was soft: "He tried to cane me that night. If it hadn't been for Miss Susie stopping him . . ."

"G.P.?"

She nodded. "Miss Susie was always good to me. It was usually the two of us against the rest of the family. Then, after what he tried to do and what he was planning, G.P. had the nerve to want me to sign a proxy for him. I wouldn't. Charles Powell, the pretty brother, came about it too."

"I know Charles," I said.

"You know Charley?" she asked, surprised. "Skid and Charley didn't get along very well. That's why Charley wasn't in Skid's will. Nobody in the family gets along. Skid and G.P. did the best. They were so much alike it was funny to watch them." She stopped and watched me. "They both liked their whiskey, they were both left-handed. When we were having trouble, Skid would always want me to sign a deed to the house so he could escrow it. After he died, then G.P. wanted me to do the same thing. He brought a deed prepared by his lawyers and said we'd put the money in escrow. Should I have signed it?"

"No. You didn't, did you?"

"No."

"That's how your father talked," Sheriff Alvie said approvingly from his position at the desk where he was rooting deep into his papers. "And that's what I told her too. G.P. had something up his sleeve, when he wanted that deed. And maybe this thing ain't done with yet." He nodded. "You look around and you'll see what they done to her. Your dad did the best he could and I know you will too."

I remembered something I wanted to clarify further.

"Tell me about this Johnathon Hartwick?" I asked. "Why was he at the house that night making drinks?"

"He sort of worked for us," she said. "He was a friend of Skid's. When Skid and G.P. weren't together, then John and Skid drank together, hunted and fished together. Mostly it was drinking. But John was a nice man. He loved flowers and plants and he'd work all day out in the yard sometimes. He passed out that night. They made him take a lie detector."

"It was the state boys who ran it, so it was probably on the up and up," Sheriff Alvie said. "John was kind of a family retainer, with Skid being his family." He frowned at his desk, baffled by the search. "He was with Skid for years. He had a bad breakdown a few months after it happened. Before the trial. He's down in the state mental hospital in Bington now." He shook his head, infuriated by the papers on his desk. "I give up. I guess you'll have to go to the clerk. I can't find those papers anywhere. It was a restraining order. Your dad looked at it and said it was okay. It didn't seem to bother him much. He acted like it was something to be expected."

I turned to the girl.

"If we take an appeal you'll most probably have to be up in women's prison for a while."

Tiny lines came around her eyes and in that moment she looked all of her years plus ten.

"I know," she said. "I keep thinking something will happen. I know if I have to go up there that I won't last very long." She looked at me and I read panic. "I didn't do it. It hurts being in here. It really hurts. Uncle Ivan's nice, but it's hard to sleep at nights. I can't eat and I feel like I'm just getting weaker and weaker. Sometime soon I'll dry all of the way out and just blow away with the wind." She nodded. "Your father knew. That's why he let them have the trial so soon."

I shook my head. "There's nothing I can do." I felt sorry for her and very unsure of myself. I was in a game that I knew little about. "It's not like I can just go over and ask them to start things again now that I'm in."

"I know. I keep thinking that if I didn't do it then someone else must have done it. Maybe . . ."

I sat and waited, but she had no ideas. At least she didn't voice any.

"You need an appeal expert," I said.

"There isn't any money for an appeal."

"Then the county will have to pay for it."

Alvie smiled at me. "If the county pays, then the county will provide the lawyer. She'll get the worst and slowest there is." He nodded. "You can bet on it."

I said: "We can't let that happen."

She shook her head and reached out and took my right hand in both of hers. "Thank you for helping," she said.

I was nervous and wanted to ask something. "What happened to your first husband?"

She shook her head, as if to clear it. "He died in an ac-

44

cident out at Powell. A conveyor carrying some heavy boxes got stacked wrong. It fell over on him."

"How long was it after his death before you met Skid?"

"Maybe three years," she said, surprised. "Why?"

"With that answer there's no good reason. Just a point I thought I wanted to explore." I looked away from her too intent eyes and then back at them. "I keep hearing the name of a Captain Ringer. How's he in this thing?"

"He isn't in it much. G.P. and Skid tried to use him as someone I was supposed to be having an affair with. G.P. had him called in by the police after Skid . . . died." She stopped and thought. "Skid used to accuse me of running around with Joe Ringer. He'd only accuse me when he was crazy drunk. Joe Ringer was just a part of our crowd. There were a lot of people who seemed to be a part of our crowd, who were always in attendance. Several of them, including Joe, were army officers from the plant. The liquor around Skid was free and there was plenty of it and people who got close to Skid sometimes seemed, in the hierarchy at the plant, to wind up with better jobs, more money." She smiled. "Skid especially favored bright young executives with handsome wives." She nodded. "His standards for what my conduct was supposed to measure up to weren't what he fancied for himself. He'd take off after anyone he wanted to chase at a party. That left me alone. A number of times Joe made an easy pass or two, but that's about as far as it went." She looked up at me and I was almost sure she was not telling me all the truth.

"What kind of pass? What did he do?"

"I guess you could say he monopolized me. He'd dance with me almost continuously. He subtly let me know he was available to take care of my needs. He wasn't nasty about it. He was just amiable and there. When we danced we'd dance close together and maybe he kissed me a time or two—nothing serious. When I wouldn't let it go any further he never got angry. He'd just go back to where it was before. And, sure, people noticed. Don't they always? There was a lot of testimony at the trial."

"I know," I said. "I heard."

"He's dead now," she said. "Both of them are dead."

I persisted: "Did the testimony show more than you're saying?"

She nodded her head slowly and her eyes stayed down. "Sure. They made it look like I spent all my time in bed with him. But I didn't. And they didn't have any direct evidence."

"All right," I said. "I'll want to go over things again with you as soon as I've had a chance to find out what I need to ask more about." I smiled encouragingly at her and let my hand lie very still in hers and she massaged it gently, without knowing what she was doing. "I'll come back later."

"All right."

I watched her silently for a moment, reluctant to end the interview.

"Do you remember me?" I asked.

She nodded, her eyes somehow shy. "Yes. I didn't know whether you remembered me. I was fourteen. I wondered for a long time after what had happened to you."

"The next day my mother left him. She took me with her."

"Oh." she said. "Of course. That would be it."

"I didn't come back for a long time," I explained. "We must have missed connections when I did come back."

She nodded again, not really forgiving me for it.

I disengaged her hands. "I'll have to go now," I said. "There's very little time and a lot to look at. I'll be back soon. Maybe I'll find something."

"All right," she said. "Look at it again for me." She got

up and nodded at me, her eyes so confident that I was sick inside. She walked away, looking back at me once. Her movements were all sweet and synchronized and I ached as I watched her. Sheriff Alvie followed her, but he made a gesture to me which she couldn't see. I thought it meant he wanted me to remain, so I returned to examining wanted posters. The deputy came back into the room, looked me over without interest, then dialed the telephone and harangued someone named Hank about a bad check.

When the sheriff came into the room again, he walked past me and sat in his chair and checked his reflection again and I waited. In the window his image was only a dim ghost and I thought he looked there at his fractured likeness because it could make him forget the aging truth.

"Kind of gets to you, doesn't she?" he asked the window and me, and then turned to survey me. The deputy had vanished again. Maybe to seek Hank.

I nodded.

"At first I wouldn't let the reporters in to see her and it was very bad for her in the news stories. She'd read them and cry. She made me let them come in and talk to her, although it took a lot from her to do it. It got better then except for the local paper. They were always bad. Powells control that one. Like they control almost everything else around here." He looked down at the backs of his liver-spotted hands. "She's real bright, Kate is. Does most of my bookwork here in the office. Keeps her occupied. I even taught her to use the radio." He shook his head. "Nice as I make it she's a bird in a small cage. She'll die quick in prison. Them people out there—damn those people out there."

"What people?"

"The Powells and their town," he said softly. "This is

their pot. Maybe Kate just somehow got caught in it. And now they've got her." He shook his head. "No one else believes that. One or more of my deputies carries out every word that passes in here." He looked at me. "I've checked it all out and there ain't anything to hang your hat on. So she wants you to take another look." He eyed me with a discouraged smile. "Know what she said when I took her back into the women's quarters?"

I shook my head.

"She said you looked like Skid must have looked when he was a young man. She said you were thinner than him, but about his size. He was a big man." He scratched his nose slyly, aware of my interest. "Where'd she know you from?"

"A long time back before we were in high school. I met her once then."

"Oh," he said. "Kid stuff."

"Yes," I said. It had been *kid stuff*.

"She's had a tough time. First husband killed before they were barely married. Then Skid came along. They had one of those marriages that keep you lawyers in business. Half love, half hate. Not really funny. I serve the court papers. Too many divorces these days. World's gone sick."

"I'll agree with that," I said. "But it's the only one there is."

"You ever met old G. P. Powell?"

"No." I never had, although I'd seen him at a distance.

"You take a careful look at him when you do. He beat this mess awfully hard. I keep thinkin' that maybe Skid was in his way somehow. G.P.'s a mean, conniving bastard. He don't think he's ever going to die." He shook his head, trying for understanding, an answer. "I got to admit that Skid and him always seemed to get along, but I can sure see G.P. killing Skid a lot quicker than I can see Kate doing it. That's all I could come up with."

"She's convicted and in, Sheriff, and he's out."

"There's that," he said. "There's always that."

I watched him and thought for a long moment. "She still thinks she's going to be freed, doesn't she, Sheriff? Haven't you told her what it will be like from now on? Didn't Pop tell her?"

"I've tried," he said defensively. "She's like a wild bird. Pen her up and she begins to die. I've had to be very careful how I treat her. She's lost maybe ten or fifteen pounds. I keep at her to eat, but she won't or can't eat much. And I guess I'm leery of really laying it onto her what prison is like. I don't know how to tell her. I think if I do it wrong she just might die. Not knowing how it's going to be, hoping for a miracle end to it, that keeps her going." He looked up at me, a long hard look. "You see, Mr. Wright, she knows she's innocent."

"Sure," I said. "Or maybe she's convinced herself that what she did wasn't wrong. And even if we win an appeal it won't be the end of it for her. If we get a reversal on legal grounds, and she makes it next time, assuming she lives that long, the newspapers and the sensational magazines will roast her for the rest of her years."

"You're not sure she's innocent," he said, dubious of me.

I watched him for a long, gloomy moment and he read the answer in my eyes.

"I've got to have facts."

His eyes were somber. "You've got a little time to acquaint yourself with the case. Go out and use it. Maybe you'll see what she was really up against and why she just might be telling the truth when she says she didn't do it."

"All right," I said.

"I can help," he said. "You tell me what you want me to do."

There wasn't going to be time to do it all. I needed to poke around the prosecution witnesses, get their smell. After that I needed to check the jury, see and hear its members. What the other side had going seemed more important to me. If there was a conspiracy of some kind in the evidence I wanted to feel it, sense it at its source. So I had to let the other thing go.

I said: "You check the jury out again. I want to know everything that happened. Find out for me. See what they debated, if anything. They weren't out long enough to do much more than elect a foreman and vote her guilty, but find out." I remembered something. "Leave out Donald Kellogg. I'll talk to him myself. I know him from a long time back. He was foreman."

"He's in a men's store now downtown. Don's Shop. On Court Street."

"Thank you."

"You'll find out," he said. "You'll see what happened. Then maybe the governor . . ." He grinned at me reassuringly, but I wasn't reassured.

"Tell me about Skid," I said. "Anything you know."

He shrugged. I was back to unimportant things, away from the conspiracy he saw. "When I was deputy awhile back we were kind of friends. We used to hunt together. I liked him then. He'd never been married and he didn't have to work at his job too hard. He always seemed to have time—time to drink with you—time to sit and talk. When I ran for sheriff he came around and tried to talk me out of it, him and Charley, and we got untracked and things got bad between us. He was on the other side of me and he told bad lies on me. Kate and him was married and having trouble by then. He'd go away for weeks at a time to hunt and fish and sulk and she was supposed to put up with it and with him. When he come back he'd expect her to be right there rocking on the porch and waitin'." He drew circles on his desk with his finger. "He wanted all of her when he was around—all her interest. He wanted to brute crush her, leave her no room to breathe in except when he breathed out. He was some kind of a cripple about her. He had her followed a lot of times. She told me he seemed upset because there wasn't anyone he could prove on her then—that was before Captain Ringer —wouldn't believe his own men, would accuse them. Once he beat one of them up and there was some smell about that, but he moneyed it over." He gave me a quizzical look. "Know what I think?"

I shook my head and waited.

"If he'd of lived I think he'd have killed her some dark rainy night. I think he'd have gotten out the very best and most treasured shotgun he owned and when she couldn't prove she loved him in all of the thousands of ways he needed, when she couldn't account for every speck of a suspect day, he'd have lovingly blown a bloody hole in her and then maybe shoved the other barrel in his own ear. He was a possessor—a cripple in the head—getting worse all of the time. He'd never really loved anyone before her and he couldn't cope with it; the fact of love was destroying him." He smiled gently at me and, for the first time, I saw that there was more than blowziness in his face. There was acquired wisdom there, too. I thought perhaps he drank too much now because he'd seen it all and never forgotten.

"Every day Skid was that much older," he said. "And yet every day there she was, young and unpossessable."

I nodded. "Jim True did the prosecuting?"

"Sure. Him and your pop were friends, but Jim did his job. Your dad said when it was over that Jim's the best trial lawyer around here. He tied it up neat, Jim did. He didn't miss a thing." He shook his head. "Then he and your dad went out and got drunk together." He gave me a piercing look. "Jim's straight, though. He don't belong to them. No more than he has to, anyhow. We all belong to them in a lot of ways. It's their town out there. They cook it and we eat it and smile about it."

"Chief Jett said something about a reward?"

He nodded. "They paid it into the police fund so as to keep it inside the law. Then the police commissioners made awards out of it. Jett got a gold medal and five thousand dollars." He smiled. "I guess it's legal that way, but it sure doesn't sound or smell any different than if they'd just give him the reward."

"I'll want an affidavit on that from you," I said.

"All right." He looked me over. "I sat in the courtroom when Judge Stickney was reading his instructions to the jury. You can read them nice and even, without a change of expression or voice and it comes out fair. What Judge Stickney did was read them with emphasis. When he had one that your dad had tendered, he'd read it so low you couldn't hardly hear it. When he had one for the prosecution he'd thunder it out. I asked Jim True about it after it was done and I think he was sort of embarrassed. Jim just shook his head."

"I'll go on now," I said. "I'll come back later," I said, feeling like I had to get out of doors. The smell of the jail had subtly gotten to me and I rose and moved toward the door.

"I knew your grandfather a long time ago," he said when I was at the door.

I stopped, ambushed a little by ghosts from the past. My grandfather was a man from my lost time, from those very early days when my mother had lived with my father.

I remembered my grandfather only as a huge man with a turnip watch on a gold chain that straddled his overalls—a farmer—a man who'd howdied everyone with dignity. Once he'd been a commissioner of the county. I'd been a small boy and we had spent much time together and been proud of one another. He'd died in the time I was first gone, when I was perhaps six or seven years old.

He said: "I knew him some. One time, right before he died, when I was deputying for Frank Stickney, he was the high judge's uncle, dead now, I made a run out there to your family place that's all cut up into town lots now. Your grandfather had a couple of them fake chimney inspectors who'd come along. He went ahead and let them do what they came for, look things over and play at working on it and him all the time sitting there big and soft-looking and smiling, talking easy to them. When they tried to get their money he refused them, but he made them think he was afraid, put them on. They got rough and he got just about twice as rough back with them as they'd ever seen. And him a sick man then. When I got out to the old place those two were laid out flat on the ground. He'd told them not to move and they wasn't trying anymore. They was right glad to see me, damned happy to be going to jail. It was the same two that had worked the county before and got some people." He shook his head. "He was a lot of man. You look as big. I hope you are." His eyes doubted it politely.

I bobbed my head to him. "Thanks, Sheriff."

Outside the heat caught me on the sharp edge of its blade again and I stopped for a moment in the blacktopped area and looked up at the sky. It was now clear and completely blue. The smog had dissipated and despite the desires of the farmers there didn't seem to be a hope of rain.

I got out a handkerchief and wiped my face. Not all of the perspiration was from the heat and sun. The woman inside had affected me. I was worried about the task ahead and full of dread of the expected outcome. I could make a few noises, but the battle was over and lost. Lovely women can die. And conviction alone might be enough to kill Kate Powell, in my opinion. Soon she would have to go to the women's prison, away from here, a bad place.

It was foolish to think about her and try to fit her into my own life. She was impossible for me. I told myself that several times. She'd been married twice, lost one, and maybe murdered the other. Our romance had been of one summer day's duration, a thing of adolescence. She was now an adult and, hopefully, so was I. She'd been maybe fourteen then, the first girl I'd ever kissed. I'd lost her the day after I'd met her. My mother had left my father.

A million things shape a person and I'd been witness to none of the sculpting since that summer day so many years ago. Those events that had happened along the way could not be rechanged. The child I'd known could be evil and sick inside, a poisoner.

I stood there, imprisoned inside myself, unable to do away with my dreams, wondering if she was another reason I'd never married. Answers had seemed simpler before I saw her.

I hadn't said anything much to Sheriff Alvie about my father's death because I'd wanted to gauge his reaction to what had happened to Pop. But he'd said nothing, indicated nothing. Maybe that meant he believed it had been an accident or illness. Maybe it meant nothing at all.

A man with familiar features came hesitantly up to me and brought me back to myself. Jim True.

He was older than my father had been. He was as thin as a piece of string, wearing a dark suit, white shirt, and a

54

bright bow tie. His shoes were dusty and so were his eyes. He'd been my father's friend for many years. They'd warred angrily against each other almost daily for those years without ever losing that friendship. I'd seen him briefly at the funeral home. He'd been one of Pop's pall-bearers.

I'd known him a little when I'd practiced with Pop and I'd liked him then. A few times he'd come north on urgent business and I'd helped him get in to see state officials without having to push around too many bodies. I knew him to be a first class trial man, like my father. They are a breed to themselves. Trial men are men who love the law, who adjust to its idiocies, shake off incompetent appellate decisions, and go on trying cases. Trial men are generally men of fair honor who exist for the courtroom, substituting its life for their own lives. Generally they are the best left of what has become a very tricky profession again in these years of the individual.

His face was open and guileless. He wasn't guileless or open. He was, I guessed, ten years or so older than my father had been. His complexion was pasty and he chewed at a cold cigar. He walked slowly, talked slowly. I'd thought, at the funeral home, that his health might be failing, for he seemed to me to be a man who was now using care in his actions and I didn't remember ever thinking that when I'd known him before.

"Hello, Mike," he said.

I shook his hand.

"Are you going to get in?" he asked.

"I guess I will, Jim."

"Good. Good. Your father and I talked about it some when it was over with." He shook his head. "Strange trial. We sort of lived to beat on each other, but we never needed any help. Your dad liked lost causes. This sure turned out to be one."

"I know that."

"They brought me the case piece by piece," he said, his eyes far away, remembering it. "It was a good case and it seemed okay to me when I was presenting it."

"I heard the judge might have taken sides in it."

He nodded. "He did do that. I don't think it would've made any difference, but he read the instructions kind of peculiar." He looked at me. "Your dad was livid." He reached a hand up and put it on my shoulder. "I thought he was going to assault old Judge Stickney, but he was too much of a lawyer for that. But he did bob up and down objecting during the instructions until Stickney threatened to find him in contempt." He smiled. "It's easy to get in contempt of Stickney. He does what he's told." His voice became contemptuous. "I wouldn't try a dogbite case in front of him on my own, but criminal cases are something else." He grinned. "He kind of set your dad up on it. In the bond hearing he acted like I was trying to crucify Miss Kate, had it under advisement for four or five days before he decided the law didn't allow a bond. That was to suck your dad in, I guess." He took his hand away. "I told your dad that a lawyer might be able to get it reversed upstate if he didn't get all of those little old women up there on the Supreme Court during their monthlies."

"I'm looking around a little."

His eyes were shrewd. "About what? About Miss Kate or your dad?"

"They say he fell down the steps there in his office," I said stolidly. "He had high blood pressure."

"Sure," he said. He looked away from me and out at the street and I thought for a moment he'd forgotten me.

56

"I know your family, Mike. I'm old enough to remember your father as a boy and I knew your grandfather pretty well. I was younger than him, but once, long ago, we raced tin lizzies down that street out there the year before they paved it. Now I'm old and your dad was getting along." He shook his head. "But I never heard him complain about dizzy spells." He stopped and a cloud passed in front of his eyes. "You come see me if you can."

"All right," I said.

He turned away abruptly, as if he'd somehow tired of me and the conversation.

I waited until he'd entered the sheriff's office and then I crossed the parking area and went into the courthouse. Inside the hall seemed cool and dark after the outside sun. I skirted the spittoons set out at the edges of the broad central corridor, and took the elevator up to the third floor and went to the clerk's office. A reluctant female deputy clerk dug me out the file I wanted to see after a few false starts. Judge Stickney had signed the order in the civil case also. It seemed he was involved in much of the business of this matter, which, I had to admit, was normal. The order restrained Kate Powell from doing anything with Skid's stock, selling it, pledging any interest in it she might have, encumbering it, voting it. It alleged the statutory irreparable harm in its affidavit signed by one G. P. Powell, verified before a notary. A bond in the amount of fifty thousand dollars, offered immediately, was a part of the file.

The order was good for ninety days. It would, I figured hastily, run out in ten more days, unless a final hearing was held.

"Note my appearance on the record," I told the clerk. "For the defendant."

"Yes, sir," she said, smacking her gum with a little more excitement.

"I'll send a formal appearance later."

I left her to her telephone, which I was pretty sure she'd use.

On an impulse, once I was out in the hall again, I walked on up a flight of steps and surveyed the courtroom. Here, my father had spent his life. Here, he'd defended Kate Powell and lost. The town must have smacked a lot of gum over that. A good dogfight could draw a crowd in Lichmont.

Judge Stickney walked in while I was standing there. Two of the town's lawyers were with him. I was sure the judge saw me, but he made no motion to show he recognized me. I was oddly satisfied about that.

I went back downstairs and out the swinging front door of the courthouse and on to my own building. The hot sun had driven the earlier crowd to shelter and only a few curious eyes watched me.

It was now close to eleven in the morning. I walked up the flight of steps and entered my office. Anne Silver, my father's secretary, nodded at me without enthusiasm.

"I was in early," I said, by way of apology. "I went to the police station and then on to the jail."

She nodded without smiling. "I suppose you talked to Mrs. Powell?"

I nodded back. "Is the file still on my desk?"

"Yes. And the newspaper would like you to call."

I started away and to my back she said: "I'll give notice now, Mr. Wright. I'll stay two more weeks—less if you can get someone sooner."

"All right," I said.

She looked away from me and at whatever was in her typewriter and went back to intently pounding at it. I went into my office and sat down in the big chair I'd assumed by right of possession only and tried to fit Anne

Silver into the scheme of things. She was a widow a few years younger than my father. He'd never remarried. She was a handsome woman with an inquiring mind. She'd cried openly at the funeral yesterday. The files seemed to be lovingly kept, although I knew my father wasn't a neat man. I wondered if he'd known she was alive and hoped that he had.

I opened the Powell file again, not really wanting to actually believe that anything was wrong. Breakdowns in the system don't really happen the way that the sensationalists would have you believe. All trials call for bias on the parts of the jurors, the witnesses, the counsel, the judge. A man reports what he remembers seeing, counsel and court interpret it, the jury interprets it again.

But there was all of that money and power and money and money.

I sighed and bent to the file. Chief Jett's name was there. He'd testified about having made the first investigation. He'd followed the ambulance to Skid's house. In notes for final argument my father had outlined his testimony. Jett had interrogated the witnesses the night Skid died and taken the original statements from those witnesses.

There was a sheaf of those statements. I started through them, counting. Eleven altogether. There was one from G. P. Powell, age seventy-six years. There was one from Dave Jordan, age thirty-five, one from Charles Powell, a long one from Johnathon Hartwick that explained his absence from the party. There was a short one from Susan Powell and a nonincriminating one from Kate Powell. They seemed, taken altogether with the rest of the statements, fairly innocuous. The only statement maker who directly accused Kate Powell of wrongdoing was G. P. Powell. No one of the other witnesses, including the other guests who'd signed statements, directly accused her of committing any offense. The statements were only showings of what they'd seen.

But then G.P. had become convinced. Maybe he'd convinced the others. Maybe also the judge and jury.

All that money.

After the statements there was an autopsy report from Dr. Sam Bush, who'd later treated my father. I skimmed through it, figuring I'd talk to him, not really overly interested as yet in the medical terminology.

Dr. Bush had been at the party, but late, after Skid was dead.

Under the statements there were copies of the many criminal documents the death of Skid Powell had caused to issue. There was an Affidavit of Probable Cause and a finding thereunder, plus a Preliminary Affidavit signed by Chief Jett, and then a copy of the indictment. There were copies of various discovery motions filed by my father in his attempt to find the limits on the prosecution's ability to prove its case. That was where, for example, he'd obtained the list of state's witnesses and copies of their statements. These days it's rough on the prosecutor who attempts to win his cases with a surprise witness. There were the pleadings and notes on the bond hearing when Kate had been refused bond by the reluctant Judge Stickney. The real mass of the file was from the trial itself.

Lawyers say they charge a thousand dollars per inch of file. If so, this file represented seven or eight thousand dollars.

Everything appeared to be competently done on both sides of the fence, prosecution and defense, if I hadn't forgotten my smattering of criminal practice and procedure. Mainly we'd represented corporations, mostly we'd closed mortgages, mostly we'd settled estates. But a lawyer is a lawyer and I had done my share of trial work.

The date of the alleged criminal act was the nineteenth of March, last past. That meant that only about three months had elapsed from the date of the crime to the time of trial. That, most surely in this age of legal dallying, was some sort of record, but was explainable because Kate Powell was in jail.

If she'd been out of jail I thought things might now be much different. If she were free there would be motions to test the sufficiency of the affidavit and the later indictment and the resulting arrest. There'd be a file full of abatements, a quash or two, motions to suppress and discover—then motions for change of venue and motions for rehearing on all the other motions.

Wear the prosecutor out is the name of the game. But delay hadn't been of much use here. It probably never was with Jim True.

My father had done legal spadework on the case itself. There were scores of written out *voir dire* questions he'd used to probe the prospective jurors, preliminary and final instructions for the jury as picked and empaneled. There were even forms of verdict for submission to that jury. My father had been a meticulous man.

On a ruled yellow pad there were pages and pages of trial notes where Pop had set down the various points of law he'd thought might be in controversy and researched them. I glanced at the collection. It would come in handy when I appealed, if I appealed. It was the last thing in the file, so I decided I'd read it through in earnest and did. There were a number of citations to cases showing that threats made before the fact were admissible; there were cites to cases involving dying declarations and expert witnesses; there were numerous citations to poison cases generally. Yet the list seemed short somehow, as if Pop had tired. He'd kept notes of time spent. His time sheets showed that the last cases on the list had been discovered and read early in the morning of the day he'd died. I shivered a little as I read that. After the trial.

G. P. Powell owned this town. My father and I were only black knights. But black knights can make things uncomfortable.

Maybe someone had swatted a fly.

It was time to start.

I dug through the somewhat dusty case reports along the walls and began to read murder cases, handling the casebooks as I thought my father would have handled them, wiping each carefully before I opened it, being easy with the brittle old pages, reading futilely along.

Some of the listed cases were in other area reporter systems, but the ones I had there in the office I heaped up about me, making notes as I went on, starting at the beginning of his list.

I was deep in when Anne Silver came to the door.

"It's noon," she said. She nodded at me, a little warmth in her eyes. "I used to have to remind him about meals when he was into the books."

"Thank you," I said. "And where's a good place for lunch these days, Miss Silver?"

She frowned. "These days I get a can of diet juice and a brisk walk in the sun. You might try the Palo Alto. It's okay."

"Thanks," I said. "I'll try it."

The Palo Alto was dark and cool after the outer heat. I sat in a booth where I could see the street. On the other side of that street industrious men washed a volunteer fire company engine. Business inside was slack.

A pert waitress wearing a mini and black panty hose came and allowed me to admire her bending to clean dishes from a nearby table. When that was finally done, she took my order curiously, with little side glances from under lowered lashes that wondered who I was and all about me. New man in small town, fairly well dressed, halfway presentable. After she'd placed my order she went to the back of the room and giggled with an older girl with long, banged hair and pointy breasts, who was dressed in the same sort of bunny-inspired costume. The world is full of disguises these days.

Soon she brought me a double cheeseburger, coffee black, and a spicy bowl of vegetable soup. We smiled happily at each other and she went on back and nudged the other waitress heavily and they giggled together again. Maybe I was the mysterious stranger who'd lead her to a split-level.

The soup was good and so was the sandwich and I ate them slowly.

I was done and lingering over the last of refilled coffee when Charley Powell came in. He shielded his eyes against the interior darkness, squinting a little, trying to find someone, and I thought maybe it was me he sought. He found me and came on back, his steps quick and light.

A few years hadn't changed him much. His hair was now a little longer and the lapels on his suit were wide and his tie covered most of the shirt which showed underneath his suit coat. He looked very good. Everything he wore seemed beautifully made. He was an extremely handsome man.

I could see the two waitresses watching him excitedly. The one who'd coquettishly served me lost her thoughts of a split-level for two and moved her dreams up into the mansion class.

I'd known Charley pretty well in law school. He was, then, one of the most competitive people I'd ever met. He wasn't overbright, but he had a desire to excel that you see in very few people—professional athletes mostly. And yet, in a world of horses and riders, he hadn't really picked his spot. He'd neither wishes to control or be controlled. He'd been a lonely person, easy enough to talk to when you were around him, but never seeking company. And all of us had known about the money, so much money.

He'd fought out the battle of law school grades and won a split decision. I'd helped him now and then. It had seemed to me, when he came out of law school, that he was still unsure, unwilling to take anything or anyone around him at face value. He'd watched the world guardedly then, his vantage point some faraway place. He'd come back to Lichmont, but they'd sent him on to the New York office, so I hadn't seen much of him after we got out of school. He'd had a minor drinking problem in those school days. It hadn't controlled him as it sometimes does control the unwary, and he seemed okay most of the time. When he was on the jug hard he hadn't been nice to be around. Few of us are.

He and I were friends in law school, but it had been a shallow thing. We'd not bothered to write each other when we were separated and, after he'd come back to Lichmont and I'd left it, I'd never called him when I'd come home to visit Pop. I'd never asked him for anything. Pop had told me that he'd cautiously helped with jury advice before the trial and that his testimony had been Kate's one bright part of that trial. Now, I wondered why he sought me out, knowing there must be a cogent reason.

I stood up and shook hands and he turned from me and smiled at my waitresses and it did more for them than a proposal of marriage from a lesser man would have done. The youngest one came toward the booth at half a gallop.

"How about another cup, Mike?" he asked. "I called your office a few minutes after you left. Your secretary told me I could probably find you here." He gripped my hand with his own slim, powerful hand, then released and sat down.

"I was going to look you up, Charley," I said. "I guess I'm going to have to take over in Kate's case. Pop said you were a help to him."

"I tried," he said. "With jury information."

"It took guts in this town."

He shook his head easily.

The nervous waitress poured us coffee and fluttered away.

He nodded at me when she was gone. "It's good to have you in town, no matter what the reason. My sympathy about your father. I know it hurts. I've been tracking you most of the morning. Tried to run you down in the courthouse, then called the jail right after you left, and missed you again at the office."

"Maybe on the Kate Powell matter?" I asked curiously.

"Not really," he said too quickly. "I guess I'm the only member of the family, except maybe Susie, G.P.'s wife, who isn't interested in lynching poor Kate. Being tolerant and unwilling to lie has made me *persona non grata* at my father's house and I've quit trying with him. He keeps screaming for blood and bones." He looked away from me. "In a way she's lucky she stayed in jail. I wouldn't want to insure her life if she was out. My father can be pretty . . . direct . . . I guess you'd say. And when he says frog around here, they're used to hopping."

"You mean he might try harming her?" I asked, not really surprised.

65

He shrugged. "Skid was his darling. He was the heir apparent, twenty-five years older than me, out of the first wife the old man had. My half sister is out of the second and I'm out of the third. My father's been married four times. Wife one was Skid's mother and so on down the line. Now he's working on number four. He's at an age where she isn't much good to him for foolish things, but he still finds ways to use this one hard." He smiled without humor. "He never divorces them—he just sort of wears them out. They say Skid was a lot like him." He made a demurring gesture. "I favor my mother."

"Four times," I murmured.

He nodded, half in embarrassment, half in jest. "The newest one is already on tranquillizers." He looked up at me, his eyes serious. "You shouldn't be in this, Mike. If he doesn't get his bucket of blood he'll take it out on you. He wields a big stick in state politics. He'll get in your way. And I hear you had it going up there."

"Someone has to help her," I said.

"I can find someone who'll take it—a good appeal man. You can get out. I'll help him."

It was attractive to think about it. I sat there and watched him and wanted to get out of it, but the face of the girl in the jail kept haunting me. And I still wasn't sure about what had happened to Pop.

"No," I said. "I appreciate it, but I guess I'll have to be the one. At least for now. I told her I'd check it out again."

"Okay," he said agreeably. "I just didn't want to see you lose something."

"Maybe I won't lose it," I said lightly. "And maybe if I do then it isn't worth having."

The waitresses were still watching him from the back of the restaurant and I ran a glance over them.

"I see you still have your charm."

He grinned boyishly. "I know a lot of girls. How about one of these nights real soon I call a couple of them and we go out on the town. I'll show you Lichmont as it is now."

"Sounds like something I ought to do if only for therapy," I said, and smiled. "Time's limited, but you're research, I guess. I'll await your call."

"How about tomorrow night?" he asked insistently.

I hesitated.

"You can pick my brain about the family if you want. Your pop did. That and the jury were what I did for him."

"Sounds good to me."

"Where are you staying?"

"I'm out at Pop's place," I said, refusing to transfer the ownership on down the line.

"Okay."

"Are you practicing any law?" I asked.

He shook his head. "Not really. I was in the New York office until about two years ago. Now I handle some of the labor stuff for the plant. Sometimes they even let me appear in minor disagreements with the federal people on our contracts with them if a sudden need arises. I've got a big office with all of the modern conveniences—hideaway bar, refrigerator, a hidden TV set that comes out of the wall, but there really isn't a hell of a lot for me to do." His eyes were restless. "When my mother died she left enough to keep me in good style. I don't need my father or the plant to exist. But I stay, hoping it will change." He looked me over. "Remember once when we were in school and we drank and talked and were going to come back here and tear this town down and rebuild it to suit ourselves—set up a partnership to end all partnerships." His eyes fell to his hands. "Well, the urge to fight the world, to change it, has sort of faded. Maybe I wouldn't even know how now.

If we have trouble the firm owns a lot of tough lawyers here and there about the country. And G.P. claims it's better for the image if outsiders handle big trouble rather than me—especially if it's federal trouble."

"Someone said there were soldiers at the plant. Is that the kind of federal trouble you mean?"

He grinned at me. "That's a leading question."

"I guess I feel like I need to know as much as possible about everything. What's going on with the government at the plant?"

"They're there for several reasons. We make a pretty full line of drugs and they check us out on those drugs in all kinds of ways—make sure the quality is as advertised, examine into our costs of making them. Plus we do some special work for the Army. I can't tell you much about that because I don't know a lot about it. It's a hush operation and I've never needed to be filled in on it." He lowered his voice a little and leaned toward me. "What they're doing out there has something to do with chemical warfare, I think. I saw an invoice once . . ." His voice trailed off. "But that was a while back."

"Oh?" I asked, interested.

"Been going on for years. Exotic stuff for some special branch of the Army. Finished now, I think."

"I wonder if they used any strychnine?" I mused.

He looked surprised. "That's an easy poison, Mike. Nothing exotic about it. It's sometimes a nerve stimulant. We use it in a few things in the plant." He nodded at me. "My undergraduate degree was in pharmacy. I know about strychnine and I brushed up on it more after the fact. We make some rodenticides for pests out there. They sometimes use it in that."

"How about trying to find out if the Army was or is using any?"

He hesitated for a minute, weighing things coolly, and then said: "I suppose I could discreetly *try* to find out."

"I'd appreciate it."

He nodded, dismissing it. "I'm about sure they aren't."

To get his attention again, I said: "Kate says she didn't poison him, Charley."

He gave me a knowing smile. "Maybe she didn't, Mike, old boy. But you've been in the practice for a while. From what you know about people accused and convicted of crime, isn't it almost a sure thing she'd deny poisoning him?"

"Not really," I said without resentment. "Lots of people have the urge to confess despite what the Supreme Court says about that urge. There's a kind of basic innocence to Kate. I don't feel that she's done anything wrong," I said, making the half lie sound sincere, waiting for his reaction.

"You mean she has a beautiful face and body and she interests you," he said, smiling broadly. "Remember that I know her. She was my half brother's wife. She also has a very bad temper at times. I've seen it in operation. My father claims she was running around with other men. There were some people who testified to it. It hurt her." He looked vaguely at his watch. "I've got to go, Mike."

"If you can help me I'd like for you to help me, Charley," I said.

He nodded quickly. "For reasons of my own I'll continue to help. Until we see who's going to wind up on top at the plant, they don't seem to want to just boot me." He grinned at me. "Another reason is that I've got a sort of stake in you. If I can keep you from getting too bloody in what's left of this fracas, then maybe you could still wind up being governor. You can then name me your administrative assistant, the high command upstate can see how amiable I am, and I can succeed you. So I'll help." His tone was light, but his eyes were serious.

"How much of the trial did you see?"

"I was in court only when I testified. I helped your dad go over the jury list and I snooped a little for him."

"Snooped?"

He nodded carefully. "He had a pretty good idea of what everyone was going to say before they said it. I gave him a few family skeletons to drag out."

"Like what?"

"Nothing of real note I guess. I told him how drunk G.P. was that night. I told him about my half sister Geneva's addiction to pills. She's one of the world's leading hypochondriacs and she's pretty well strung out these days. She needs something in the morning to get her moving, something to keep her head high, something else for the times she gets too far out, then something else for sleeping." He shook his head. "By the time your dad got done with her on the stand, she really didn't do much damage. The damage was cumulative."

"I need to know anything else you can think of about your family."

"Ask away."

"Tell me a little about Dave Jordan."

"My sister Geneva's husband?" He seemed surprised. "He's nothing extraordinary. I guess the biggest thing you can say about him, other than that he runs the plant, is that he's my sister's husband." He nodded. "I think she deserves Dave and he deserves her. She isn't a happy woman and she has her problems, like I said before. And Dave is competent enough in a dull way. We don't progress much, but we've made money with Dave at the helm. He calls a conference every time we sell an aspirin. He's careful and cautious. He has some stock and options on more." His eyes fell from mine. "Someday he and Geneva will boot me out or vice versa. That day can't come too soon for me. I'd rid myself of him without a qualm. But I think it says something about him that he doesn't do that with me. I'll be around until they are sure there's nothing I can do to cut them up and positive that they know everything I know. That's why they brought me back from New York."

"Were they at the afternoon picnic the day Skid died?"

"Sure. It wasn't really a picnic, just a family get-together around the pool at G.P.'s. Food and drink and some family bickering between Skid and G.P. Then the party, including Kate, later."

"Bickering about what?"

"The usual. Running the plant. Who should move up, who should be moved out. It wasn't anything special and I can't remember anything that happened there that would be of interest to anyone else now." He looked at his watch pointedly.

He got up when I nodded at him. He said: "Again, I'm sorry about your dad. He was a first class man."

"Thank you," I said. "And thanks for helping him and me."

I paid while he smiled over my shoulder and we left the enchanted waitresses to an afternoon of air-conditioned comfort and hot flashes.

Outside the sidewalk was fairly crowded with people hurrying back to work. Some of them watched us curiously. Other eyes seemed hostile.

He said: "I'll call you tomorrow afternoon with big plans. An evening for your memory book."

I nodded.

"And watch yourself," he said softly.

"I'll try."

"Did you ever think you dad might not have fallen down those steps?" he asked.

"I've considered it."

"He was buzzing around asking a lot of questions. Maybe he got on someone's nerves." He smiled at me and turned away and got into a sleek black Continental Mark with a tire mount on the rear. He made a U turn in the street, waved at whoever was watching, then sped away.

Across the street the men from the fire company watched the disappearing car.

"That was Charley Powell," one of them said proudly to the others, still staring.

"Yeah? I bet he gets plenty in that car," another said enviously. "I guess even that hot, jailbird sister-in-law of his. I hear they . . ." He saw me staring, recognized me, and dropped his voice.

I eavesdropped hopefully, but the voices remained low, so I reluctantly walked on back past the courthouse and on to my office, moving quickly. Outside, on the lawn of the courthouse, the loafers had arrived early for the afternoon shift. The pecking order for the day was being decided and they eyed me as I walked by. I was hurrying and I knew they'd discuss that, for it was a violation of their rules, but they appeared tolerant about it for now and smiled without much malice and went back to knife trading.

I told myself, as I walked, that I'd never believed in street gossip.

The steep steps up to the office were now bathed in the hot light of early afternoon. I checked them again in the surer light. Surely Pop had walked up and down them fifty thousand times. I looked them over closely. They were wood and they were old, but the rubber insets seemed in good shape. Two lights burned above the steps and a third receptacle was empty, a wire dangling untidily from it.

If someone had aided Pop down those steps I'd have to chance on him/her. Besides, there was Kate Powell to consider. But by sticking around and agitating things the odds might improve.

Inside the office Anne Silver was pounding a fair rhythm on her typewriter. Two gentlemen waited. The larger of the two wore a large belly and a uniform with bright, insignificant ribbons and silver maple leaves. The smaller man was dressed in civilian clothes.

I thought I read a warning in Anne's eyes.

She said: "This is Mr. Jordan. David Jordan." She nodded at the other man, the one in uniform. "And this is Colonel Uhland."

I shook hands. Jordan examined me through the microscope of his thick glasses. They were deeply tinted and it was difficult to read any expression in the eyes behind them.

The colonel had a beefy body and face. He was big, almost as big as me. Something was biting at him. He seemed very tense and irritable.

Both men appeared to be in their mid forties. To the best of my knowledge I'd never seen either of them before, although I remembered vaguely when Jordan had come to town years back, before he married a Powell.

Jordan was about as Charley Powell had advertised him. He was medium height and build, with a receding hairline of the kind that comes to a front point. His hair was sparse gray and brown. His suit was expensive cloth, but the cut of it did little for him. I believed he was a man who'd spent his lifetime being a member of the crowd—someone few remembered—but a man who could be trusted to head up a fund drive or count the money after church. Now it wasn't that way anymore. He had power now that he ran Powell. He also radiated uncertainty, unsureness of that power.

I led them into my office. Jordan waited politely until I pointed to a chair, but Colonel Uhland didn't bother with formalities. He took the nearest chair and glared at me from it, seeming to want trouble.

"Maybe we shouldn't be here," Jordan said, his tone belying it.

"Tell him, Dave," the colonel rumbled. "Let's say what needs to be said. And get out."

Jordan looked coolly at the bigger man and the colonel subsided for the moment.

"You are in charge of the military out at Powell?" I asked the colonel.

He nodded, his eyes murderous as they contemplated me. He said insultingly: "I'll sure be damned glad when I've seen the last of the Wright plague in this town. Maybe then I can get back to some soldiering."

I smiled at him. "I don't know where that came from, Colonel. Far as I'm concerned you can get back to soldiering anytime. Right now if you want. I didn't even know who you were until just this instant."

"Your dad did," he said, and sneered. "And I knew him —to my sorrow."

I felt something cold gather in me and I wondered how it would feel to tear a piece of him away from the rest.

Jordan stepped into the breach. He said: "We're sorry about your father."

I nodded and saw Colonel Uhland make an impatient gesture. He was going to see how far he could go.

It seemed like a good time to draw lines. I said: "Mr. Jordan—you are welcome to remain. I'm assuming you

74

came here for something." I nodded. "Whatever it is I'm willing to discuss it." I turned to the other man. "You will remove yourself from my office, Colonel. I don't know who pulled your chain, but I don't want to hear or see you flushing in here." I got up. "Now," I said. "Immediately!"

He got up and for a quick moment I thought he was going to contest matters, but he looked at Jordan and he must have read something there I couldn't read.

"I'll see you again," he said harshly.

I nodded. "I hope so. I'm available."

Jordan sucked calmly at his lips and we watched the colonel leave, banging the outer door hard.

Jordan smiled at me. "He's a direct man. He's taken a lot of interest in this. I wouldn't anger him too much. He's got a black belt in karate."

I remembered the colonel's girth. "Maybe he should use his black belt to hold things together in the middle."

"I'm sorry it started this way," Jordan said. "But there are a lot of rumors around town. I'm afraid they've irritated the colonel. He retires next year and will come to work for us then. It's been said, for example, that you intend to tamper with the time set for sentencing."

"That's possible."

He shook his head, smiling. "We checked on that. The judge sets the time. My understanding is that the time as now set is definite."

It was, unless I could talk the judge into a change, which, remembering him, seemed a remote chance.

"Perhaps that's so," I said, not seeing any advantage in admitting it.

He shrugged. "I'll have to take my own legal advice about that, but there are more serious rumors. You work for the governor. I'm informed that what's been done down here may very well be quickly undone at the state level."

"Now wherever could a rumor like that start?" I asked.

He shook his head and I got a view of his eyes as the light hit his glasses just right. They were intelligent eyes, with small worry lines radiating from the folds of flesh around them. He put a hand in his jacket pocket and measured the distance out to Anne Silver's desk, trying to decide whether there was a chance she could hear us. The careful computer inside his head decided and he leaned toward me, his voice low.

"It could ruin the company," he said. "If she were let off now the repercussions could easily ruin the company." He nodded primly. "I think everyone would be better off, including you, Mr. Wright, if sentence were passed at the set time and there were no further maneuvering for a while. I didn't come here to ask you to do something which will jeopardize your client, but the company would be better off, healthier, if everything could be done with and quiet before the annual meeting." He looked up, his face seemingly earnest. "Please understand me, Mr. Wright: I don't really care what finally happens to Kate. If you can get her off, then hooray for both of you. The difficulty is that the company is in an awkward position just at this moment. We lost income last year and the stockholders are . . . restive . . . I believe you'd say. The case has been a sensational one and every time a newspaper prints a word about it they also print something about Powell Chemicals. Our annual meeting is in a few weeks." He nodded carefully. "I think all of us in management would like to see a touchy period behind us." He looked me over again carefully. "I wouldn't want you to come into the case now, tamper about with it, and cause us harm without good reason. I'm sure your father wouldn't have wanted that either. He lived here. He knew the harm that can come to the town if the company is affected badly."

I sat there for a moment, exploring things. I was a little angry and more surprised, but I did my best to keep it from showing. I explored for the possibility of advantage.

"I don't want to do anything that my father wouldn't do. Trouble is that it's such a very short time for me to be involved and to be satisfied about what took place, about fairness really," I said, keeping my voice reasonable. "I'd thought to ask for more time and ask the governor's help if necessary, but perhaps there's a way it just might work out so that any tampering, as you put it, might not be necessary." I nodded at him. He watched me attentively. "I want to take a look around, more to placate Kate and Sheriff Alvie than for any other reason. I want to be able to get at the important witnesses who testified for the state, see what I need to see, examine things without having to do a lot of chasing. If I'm impeded then I'll use whatever remedies are available to me, perhaps even seek some help at the top level." I stopped for a moment and then went on: "Maybe you can stop that, maybe you can't." I shrugged. "Basically what I'm interested in is obtaining enough evidence to satisfy myself that all the protestations I've heard from my father's client are just the things you normally get from a loser. But Kate keeps repeating she didn't commit the murder and keeps wanting me to look things over again. I'm assuming that such a rehash will at least partially satisfy her." I shook my head. "And so far I haven't a shred of anything contrary to the verdict or any evidence of a direct nature that the verdict was arrived at contrary to the law and evidence. Oh, there was pressure, but so what? Pressure is normal. What I want from you, in return for a promise of no immediate undercover work upstate by me for Kate Powell, is help in examining into the trial, the key witnesses, the places involved in Skid's death."

He watched me and I wondered if he'd called the governor. Surely he must have called him and gotten an answer that wasn't good enough. And I knew that such an answer didn't mean, as he was assuming, that the governor would help me.

He was silent for a long moment. Finally he said: "I guess what you're asking is all right. As far as I know everything was fair enough about the trial and you can certainly look at anything you want if it will help smooth things over." He nodded. "Sure, you can," he said, his voice more positive and confident.

I tried to keep exultation out of my face and smiled at him disarmingly. "Were you present when Skid died, Mr. Jordan? And did you testify?"

"Dave," he said magnanimously. "Please call me Dave." He nodded. "I was around. So was Colonel Uhland. Both of us testified, although I'm sure the record will show you my—our—testimony was fairly innocuous."

"Tell me what you remember seeing the night that Skid died," I asked.

Again, for a long, careful moment, he thought about it. "I didn't see much, I'm afraid. I was here and there talking with some of our people about various problems at the plant. When the tumult started I came back in. I think that Colonel Uhland and I had been outside discussing a cost problem in his area." His voice was matter-of-fact. "He left. I came back in."

"Let's see—that would have been in March. Wasn't it pretty cold to be outside?"

"It wasn't warm," he said.

"How'd you get along with Skid personally?"

He smiled. "Just fair, I guess. He ran the plant by instinct and he wasn't too bad at it. We had a lot of unnecessary expense, but we made money. I'm a detail man myself. I think it would be correct to say that our methods differed when we worked together. Some of the clashes we had were quite unfriendly. He was—emotional."

"And his death pushed you to the top."

"I suppose," he said stolidly. "I'm not really comfortable in what I'm doing now. I was happy in my old job and I made about the same kind of money then. There were problems, but not so many of them." He looked away from me and took some time and considered things again. I had a sudden empathetic feeling with him. Skid's death had pushed him into the pilot's seat, yes, but only as my father's death had pushed me where I was now. Fate had made the choice for both of us, unless Jordan had helped his fate along.

He nodded. "Some days I'd give it all up for a dime. But the plant has to go on of course. I guess the country needs us. I know this town needs us. There has to be a person who handles the running of the plant. Now that I'm in that position, that place of control, then I suppose I resist efforts to remove me. That's why I'm here more than any other reason, why I brought Colonel Uhland along. Kate's immediate sentencing can help alleviate some of our problems."

"How?" I asked sharply, not really understanding. "Why?"

He said reasonably: "We don't have an enormous group of stockholders, Mike. We're not listed on any of the exchanges. Our stock sells only over the counter. It's a small float. There are considerably more shares of stock outside the family than inside it. When Skid died it was about like throwing a stone in a still pond. The fight had already begun then and there were quick ripples. The story circulated that Skid had siphoned off a great deal of money by way of switching it around in some complicated fashions from the federal projects we're involved in."

"Oh, I see," I said, trying to do so.

"The federal people checked us out clean and passed on what their examiners found, but a large corporation isn't always believed. The rumors haven't abated. We know there's a group trying to move in and take over the company, willing to use whatever means are available. Many of our stockholders have received attractive offers for their stock from a group calling themselves the 'Medical Consultants.' There's a magazine publisher in Hartford City who's ostensibly the head of the group. We still think we have the upper hand, but our position is shaky. It's hard to plan for the future when we don't know what will be happening in three weeks at the stockholders' meeting. The new rumors that are going around are that we know that Kate didn't kill Skid and that she'll never be sentenced —that we've fixed the case to help our cause. They say that if Kate could vote her shares she'd vote us out. Maybe she would at that, but there's an injunction. Your coming into it hasn't helped things. You have political connections that lend credence to wild rumors. Thank God there isn't much time left until sentencing."

"Who's really behind the Medical Consultants group?" I asked.

He shrugged, but I caught a glimpse of his eyes again and I thought he knew.

"In your opinion did Skid's poison come from the plant?"

"I said in court that it probably did come from there." He hesitated. "I didn't testify about it, but the testimony showed that one of the Army people at the plant, a Captain Joe Ringer, was most friendly with Kate. More than

80

friends. And strychnine wouldn't be difficult to obtain out there."

"Is the Army using it in whatever it is they're doing out there?"

"Not specifically to the best of my knowledge, but I guess there could be some around and available." He stopped. "The problem about identifying it was the missing glass. The various experts who testified, from Doc Bush on, could state about finding the strychnine in Skid upon autopsy, but they couldn't testify from what sort of compound it had come." He nodded to himself. "My bet would be a pesticide. Strong enough to do the job without requiring a lot of refining. But it would take a lot of it that way."

"How much?"

"For as much as was in him maybe as much as a quarter or maybe a half an ounce." He examined his hands. "But of course she could have had the refined stuff."

"Wouldn't someone have had to supply it to her?"

"Why?" he asked. "She's a bright woman. She could have figured it out some way—gotten it in some fashion. She would never even have had to come near the plant. Skid never let her come around it anyway, so I guess she didn't get ahold of it that way."

"She never was around the plant at all?"

"That's right. She just wasn't allowed. She got whistled at once way back around the plant and so Skid ordered her not to come around anymore. I never saw her or heard of her being around after that from maybe four years back." He nodded at me. "Your dad asked me all this at the trial. You'll find it in the testimony."

"What are you doing out there that has an Army colonel so interested in your business that he's automatically angry at me?"

"Research," he said shortly. "Or we were."

I raised my voice a little, frowning. "I think I'd like to know in what fields, Dave."

He said reluctantly: "Chemical warfare and some of its allied fields. And that's about as much as I can tell you even now."

"Germ warfare?" I persisted.

He shrugged. "They've stopped all work in that field for now. But it had to move someplace a few years back and I guess the powers thought Powell and Lichmont might be a good place. Small town and all."

"Any poisons that might imitate strychnine?"

"Most poisons imitate each other to some extent if they are lethal. But the toxicologists testified that what killed Skid was simply strychnine."

I decided there might be a better source to pursue answers on that. I could talk to Dr. Sam Bush.

"How did your wife take Skid's death?"

"Skid was one of the very few people that Geneva was interested in. I thought for a while she was going to go the way that John did."

"You mean Johnathon Hartwick?"

"Yes. Skid helped him get a parole. Bad checks, I think. They hunted together, fished together, chased women. For a lot of years. John was a most charming man, very much like Skid. The poor man had some kind of a mental breakdown after Skid died. He's in the state hospital in Bington."

"I heard that."

He got up from his chair and nodded peremptorily. "I've got to be getting back to the plant."

"I'd like to talk to your wife," I said.

He smiled. "So would I sometimes." He shook his head. "I'm being irrational, Mr. Wright. Geneva and I aren't going so well these days. With her, you're on your own." He nodded. "I'll help you any other way I can, but my wife doesn't choose to do all of what I tell her these days."

That was interesting and I filed it away for perusal later.

"I'd appreciate it then if you'd call your father-in-law, G. P. Powell, and tell him I'd like to talk to him later this afternoon."

"You're being foolish of course," he said wearily. "But I'll call him and if I ask him to then maybe he'll talk to you—I should say yell at you." He nodded to himself. "I'd be careful with him if I were you."

I nodded and that encouraged him to go further.

"Maybe I ought to be able to tell him a little about what you want to discuss with him?"

"I really would like to talk with both G.P. and his wife," I corrected. "Just tell them the agreement we've made." I gave him my best smile. "Say I want to go over the testimony they gave. Last-minute sort of thing."

"She didn't testify," he said.

"I'd still like to talk to her. She was there."

"Okay, but take it easy around G.P.," he said anxiously, with a hint of warning in his eyes. "He has a lot of friends. A man who got things started wrong with him . . ." He stopped and considered me and decided he'd said enough.

"I'll take it easy," I said. I gave him my best doubtful look. "Maybe we just should call the whole thing off. I'll do what I can for Kate and no one down around here will have to put up with my irritating questions." I wondered if he'd sense now that my hole card was no higher than a three. It seemed apparent to me.

He didn't sense it. "No," he said hastily. "I'll call G.P. and he'll talk to you. Just don't start trouble."

I nodded. The police chief had told me that also. I wondered what kind of trouble I wasn't supposed to start. I wondered where I could find some of it.

"What sort of trouble do you mean?" I asked innocently.

"Just trouble," he said with minor heat. "No one starts trouble here in Lichmont. The unions used to try." He nodded and fell silent again and I remembered a few times when I'd been around and the unions had tried to infiltrate Powell. Things hadn't been very calm. The plant still was nonunion.

"I talked to the governor about you today," he said. "We were pretty close during the last campaign. I understand that you and he are close also. He told me he hoped you'd have a future in politics."

I smiled to myself. Now, I could maybe figure why he had a case of the jumps. He'd tried to put the hammer on the governor, find out how I was wired and what I could do, and he'd been unable to get a clear answer. That had brought him running to me. And I had a sudden hunch about the opening scene in my office. They'd played bad guy and good guy for me, then given me my choice. If I folded to belligerence, that was one thing; if I didn't they hadn't lost much.

"Just remember that I've made you no direct promises about this, Dave," I said, my voice as promising as I could make it, one Rotarian to another.

"Sure," he said, reading me and smiling at me.

"And thanks for the help. I hope you'll speak to the colonel about not feeling too badly toward me. I've been under a strain."

He nodded and moved quickly to the door, a colorless, careful man and yet I was impressed by him and I hadn't expected to be impressed.

Outside, in the hall, I heard the colonel greet him cheerily and, together, I heard them tramp down the hall.

Anne Silver sat at her typewriter, watching me.

"Hearing you out here your voice sounded just like your father's," she said plaintively, and nodded. "He kept saying someday you'd come back here. What a shame it had to be like this."

Depression returned. I'm good at popping balloons, but incompetent at raising them. I looked around the office and it seemed like an unreal place to me, someplace that I didn't need to be. I'd worked for a long time to get up or down to where I was. Now I was on the threshold. It was really a time for soft words and a bowed head and the road back north.

I said: "We had a relationship that made it so that I couldn't come back until I'd proved myself, Miss Silver." That really wasn't it at all. We'd seen things differently and the operation of Wright and Wright had been more on a parental basis than a legal one. But I finished: "He kept my name on the door so I could come back someday and we got along after I left." It sounded lame and it was, but it was as much as I was going to say to her.

She nodded, perhaps partly convinced that I wasn't as bad as what she'd believed. Her loyalties still lay with him, but he was dead and she was rudderless just now, wanting someone to steer the boat for the short, uncomfortable two weeks' time she had promised because of him.

She said for conversation: "The typing you hear is me composing letters to his various clients telling them not to come in until we notify them. Give you time to decide what you want to do."

I nodded. "That's a good idea. One other thing—I don't want or need to talk to any newspapermen. If any of them come here you know nothing—you don't even know whether I'm in the Powell case."

She nodded. "I'll try." She watched me for a minute.

85

"Your father was sick when he lost her case. He came in that day like a rain cloud. He slammed the door to his office and I heard him banging around in there cursing. And I think it took something out of him."

"Did he ever act like he was sick over a period of, say, the past few months?"

She shrugged. "Doc Bush was giving him some medicine." She opened a drawer and pawed around and came out with a bottle. "Here it is. I kept the bottle out here on my desk to remind him."

I took the bottle. I sniffed at the odorless pills inside it, examined the legend on the front of the bottle. It wasn't from a drugstore, but appeared to have been given to Pop directly from the doctor. All I knew was that he was supposed to take the pills as needed.

I put the bottle in my pocket.

"What now?" she asked.

"I'm going out to Mr. G. P. Powell's house."

Her eyes got bigger. "Your father went out there after the trial," she said. "It was the afternoon before he fell down the steps."

"Tell me all that you know about Pop's fall," I said.

"I don't know much about it. By the time I came to work that morning, the ambulance had already come and taken him to the hospital. The janitor said he found him at the bottom of the steps. He said your father smelled of liquor." She watched me. "I told you all that I knew when I saw you that first day at the hospital."

"I thought maybe you might have talked to the janitor and he might have added something."

She nodded. "He's been in once. He said that he guessed the last light on the stairs was out again."

"Burned out?"

"Yes. I asked him. There are supposed to be three of

86

them, but one of the receptacles never has worked since I've been here. Another bulb burned out a few weeks back and that left one. I guess your father tried to go down the steps after the last one blew and just fell. He liked to be here late and come early in the morning when he was working on something. The stairs could be pretty dim even with one light until the sun got up. The janitor saved me the light bulb; thought maybe your dad would like to see it if he recovered." She reached down and rummaged through her bottom desk drawer. "Here it is." She handed it to me and nodded. "I think he wanted your dad to sue the owners. They don't give him much to operate with. He said there's insurance."

I looked at the bulb and shivered a little. The glass part was slightly loose in its metal screw end. That *could* have happened when it was taken out by the janitor. Maybe.

She watched me inspecting the bulb. "He said it was loose like that when he found it. Kids, maybe. They come in during the day on the stairs, reach up and give the bulb a good twist and the air hits the element and it blows when someone flips the switch."

"Probably right," I said. "I'll go now."

She held up her hand, stopping me. "Try to talk to Susie Powell at G.P.'s place. I used to work with her over in the clerk's office before she married that nasty old man. She's nice and she likes to tell the truth. She used to get herself in all kinds of trouble in the clerk's office with that." She smiled, remembering. "She's almost too honest. You may not be able to get her to talk to you, but you can pretty much believe what she tells you if you get anything out of her. But that's only if G.P. isn't right there slobbering on her when you talk to her. She seems to get very nervous when he's around. I think she might be afraid of him. He's a mean old man. I know him. If he's close by then just forget it."

"How long have they been married?" I asked.

"Couple of years. Plenty long enough for her to get right sick of it."

"How do you know that?"

"I just know. We've been friends for a while. I had lunch with her not too many months ago, right before Skid died. She looked bad then. I asked her right out how things were going, after I shoved a martini or two into her. Like I said, she's compulsively honest. She told me she was going to leave him, but she never has." She gave me an eloquent nod. "Maybe things are improved. There's all that money and Susie likes money. I've only seen her at a distance recently. I think she's maybe avoiding me. Sometimes she acts like she's drunk or something. Maybe he's got her on some kind of drugs, like Geneva."

"How like Geneva?" I asked, wanting to hear the story again.

"That was catty," she answered. "People out at the plant say Geneva is sort of a pill head. But I don't really know anything."

"Thanks," I said.

She smiled at me. Somehow, in the giving and taking of information, a small hole had opened in the dike of resentment she owned for me. I was glad.

"I'll try to see her," I said.

"You know where the house is?"

I nodded. "I think so. It's on the lake. I'll go there now and tomorrow maybe you could show me Skid's house?"

"All right," she said, visibly pleased. She consulted her notes. "One more thing that I forgot and shouldn't have forgotten is that Mr. True called. He's going to be out of town the rest of today, but wants to talk to you tomorrow if it's convenient."

Donald Kellogg, who'd been foreman of the jury and whose name Pop had circled, had a clothing store on Main Street. I walked down there, trying to stay in the shade, feeling myself sweat. By now I believed most Lichmonters knew who I was. I also got the impression that many of the people of the town would just as soon not have me around. Here and there a face turned quickly away when I was noticed. I could stop now and then and see eyes on me, see heated discussions being carried on. Maybe I was slightly paranoid, which was possible.

I smiled broadly at everyone. It didn't cost anything.

The windows of the Kellogg store were strewn with items of clothes. The brands were cheap and second rate. A store dummy, suffering the outrage of an ancient hair style, guarded the larger of the two windows. It wore bright, flared pants and a body shirt.

Inside, a middle-aged lady waited on a lone customer. The lights were dim and there didn't seem to be anyone else around. At the back of the store there was a flight of stairs that led up to a second-floor loft, unwalled, partially visible from below. I stopped near the lady clerk and waited while she boredly explained the price of various types of undershorts to a long-haired teen-age boy, who was embarrassed by what was being reported.

He scuttled gratefully away finally, vowing he'd return. The lady clerk watched him with eyes that didn't believe him, and then turned to me.

"Donald Kellogg?" I inquired.

"Up at the top of the stairs," she said curtly.

"Thank you." I went on back and up the stairs. At the top there were some more tables where things appeared to be jumbled. Away from that, lit only by the brilliance of one naked bulb, there was an old desk. Donald Kellogg sat at the desk. I recognized him from many years back in time, more because I knew it was him than from inspection. His chest seemed too narrow, his beam too broad.

I walked on back. He was working on some figures in a book on his desk, but he paused when I drew near.

"We're not taking on any new lines," he said. He smiled at me without hope or hate. "Or maybe you're here on those uniforms for out at Powell?"

That captured my interest, but I shook my head. He stared at me, still without recognition.

"I remember an afternoon I rode my bicycle across your garden," I said.

His eyes squinted down a little. "Mike Wright," he said carefully. "I heard you was in town. I didn't get down to the funeral home to see your dad, sorry to say. He was a good man." He shook his head. "I've still got a scar over my eye you gave me." He grinned and it seemed to me that I saw a little of the old Kellogg in his eyes, some vestige of that good youthful madness. He came up from the chair and shook my hand. "I'd hate to try you now," he said, looking up at me.

"Good to see you," I said.

"I heard about you taking her case over. It was on the radio," he said. He looked away from me so that I couldn't see his eyes. "Your dad was in once after the trial." He smiled at the wall. "I never could figure why."

"Oh?" I asked. "Some mentions in his notes made me think you'd told him a few things about the jury deliberations."

"I didn't tell him anything," he said quickly.

"It didn't take your jury long," I said.

"She was guilty," he said. He looked away from me and around his dark and aging store. "All the people on the jury knew about Kate and where she came from. I could tell after the first day of testimony how it was going to go. Your dad was wasting his time and ours."

"You mean you discussed it before all of the evidence was in?"

"Why do you ask that?" he asked guardedly.

"No reason. Did you?"

He shook his head. "I guess not. We did it the way Judge Stickney told us to do it."

"Are you doing some business with them out at Powell now?" I asked.

He faced me squarely. "Yes. I'd sure hate to lose it. I fought a long time to get some of it. And business around this town ain't so good, Mike. I bought in with old man Dobbie and now he's been sick and about to die for almost a year. There's only me and Mrs. Lutes downstairs doing it all except the extra high-school help at Christmas." He stared hard at me. "I'd just rather not say anything more about it. It's done with for me. Leave me out." His voice took on a plaintive note. "For old times' sake."

I looked at him. His jowls were heavily fleshed and he was building a pot around his middle. The daily act of living and scheming to live had taken all of what he had been before away from him. I nodded at him without assurance and moved a little closer. He closed the books he'd been working on and stepped in front of me with a weak smile.

"It's good to see you though, Mike." He touched my shoulder with a tentative hand. "I hear you're big in politics upstate." He bent forward, nodding at me, and in the gesture I could see where his hair had grown thin and something inside me felt my own age and I was sad remembering two boys who'd fought exuberantly, two boys who'd cut their fingers with razor blades and bled a little into each other—so they could be brothers, and who could no longer be truthful. I knew he was lying to me and I had a sudden desire to hurt him. He was living in his world without regard to anyone else. I knew that if I could rend him and it would help Kate that I would do it without feeling. I turned away, thinking he might read my eyes as I'd read his.

"I just thought I'd drop in," I said to the wall. "While I'm here maybe I could get you to fix me up with a few shirts. I was traveling light."

He nodded. "Sure, sure. Old Red will fix things up for his buddy, Mike. Blood brother Mike," he said, remembering. "And when things cool down a little around town I want you to come out and meet my Nelda and the kids. But not right now. The talk out there is still ugly."

I nodded, knowing that I was an adult and that I would never be a child with him again.

"Thanks, buddy," I said.

In Lichmont, in the time of my early years, there once lived a bright land speculator named Diddberg. He bought about five hundred acres at the east edge of the town, hilly land, heavily timbered. The farmers who sold it to him joked about "Crazy" Diddberg and how he wouldn't be able to raise hell on the land with two hot ladies of the evening and a gallon of whiskey. Diddberg raised a dam instead between the two major hills. He bulldozed out the bottom and let a big quiet lake fill. That lake I remembered with nostalgia.

Diddberg sold a few of the lots around the lake to people who liked the trees and the water enough to pay his high asking price. That repaid most of his investment. Thereafter, he sat on the rest of the land.

When he died he cannily left a part of the lake front to the city of Lichmont, "to be converted into a public beach."

The city named it Diddberg Beach and it was for all time from that named "Diddle Beach" to the young and interested.

His heirs sold the rest of the land, after subdividing it again and naming the division "Lake Acres." When I'd left prices were steep and, according to what Pop had told me since, they'd grown steeper.

The senior Powell's home occupied about five hundred feet of water frontage. I estimated land value at about seventy-five thousand. The house itself was well camouflaged by bushes and trees and was invisible from the road. The entrance way was at the end of an ornate iron fence. A discreet sign announced "Powell, G. P."—nothing more.

I drove my dusty LTD in and parked it in front of a brick and stone home that was complex and sprawling, with three distinct wings. From a fenced yard three alert Dobermans watched me carefully, their tongues lolling in the heat, their coats glossy.

I rang a doorbell and heard the chimes inside. In a while a handsome black maid opened the heavy door and blinked warily out at me and the sun.

"Yes, mister?" she asked.

"Is Mr. Powell at home?"

"No, sir."

"How about Mrs. Powell?"

"Would she be expecting you?" she asked, her eyes suspicious.

"I don't know," I said. "Mr. Jordan might have called her."

"He did call a while ago," she said, and looked me over with more interest.

"Tell her that I'm Kate Powell's new attorney. It's about Kate."

She tentatively decided for me. "All right. I'll tell her.

You come on into the hall." She opened the door and stepped back. "What's your name?"

"Mike Wright." I saw she recognized the name.

I followed her in and waited. The entrance hall was several stories high. An immense lamp, bigger than me, hung down from the ceiling. Gold-bordered mirrors, ornately made, showed me that there was a little gray at my temples. The floor beneath me was slate.

I heard the maid open and close doors and, after a while, I heard her steps returning. She smiled at me.

"She'll see you," she said, surprised about it.

I let her lead me back through sliding doors to a huge pool area with a sliding roof, rolled back now. Something chemical had changed the color of the water to an antiseptic blue. A woman in an abbreviated suit churned out of the water at the sun end of the pool and looked me over. The Dobermans came to a low fence by the pool and watched me as if I was dinner.

She said a soft word to them and they seemed to relax a little, but I moved slowly.

I thought the woman was a little on the far side of forty, but she was defending against it and doing a good job. Her skin, when she moved near, was satiny and soft-looking. A curl of dark hair escaped from under her cap and she brushed water from it. Her eyes were china blue, a doll's eyes. Her figure was extremely good, without sags. She was a very handsome woman.

She took a large bath towel from a folding chair and swaddled part of herself inside it. She nodded carefully at me and said to the maid: "Go do what I said to do."

The maid nodded cryptically and went away.

"She said you were Kate's lawyer?"

"Yes, I am. Mike Wright. Dave Jordan was supposed to call and say I'd be out."

94

"He just did so within the last few minutes." She shook her head. "I wasn't expecting you so soon." She held out a hand that shook slightly. "I'm Susan Powell, Mr. G. P. Powell's wife." She sat down in a folding chair and motioned me to do the same in another. "How can I help you?"

"The sentencing is next Monday. Your husband was one of the main witnesses who testified for the state. I promised Kate that I'd try to go over the case for her, see if my father might have missed anything, or if anyone has had any second thoughts since the trial." I smiled at her, making it all half a joke.

She seemed hesitant still about talking to me. Her eyes watched the door.

"Anne Silver said I should try to talk to you," I said in a low voice. "She said you'd give me the straight of what you saw that night—that I could believe you."

"Sometimes I miss Annie," she said. I thought she relaxed a little, but it was such a small thing that I wasn't really sure.

"Tell me about what happened that night?" I asked, while her eyes were still soft.

"You mean the night that Skid died?" she asked.

"Yes. That night."

"I'd rather not talk about it." She shook her head. "Mr. Powell will be along soon. You should talk to him. It isn't proper that I talk about it."

"Why not? Didn't Dave Jordan tell you to talk to me?"

She nodded, but her eyes seemed stubborn.

"Then tell me about the party, about what you saw," I insisted.

She said: "It was just a party. Skid had a lot of parties. This was another one." She shivered, remembering. "It was cold outside and there was some snow, I think. There

95

were a lot of people around and they were drinking and dancing. People were having fun. Kate and Skid had been having some trouble before at the picnic. He thought she was running around on him with a soldier out at the plant." She smiled and shook her head. "I know she wasn't doing much of that. I told them all that night." She looked away. "The soldier's dead now."

"Who did you tell?"

She was vague. "Whoever would listen. Dave and his wife, Mr. Powell, Skid." She nodded. "A lot of people must have heard me. Skid was picking at her and starting it all over again. Mr. Powell wasn't any help."

"Who do you mean when you say 'Mr. Powell'?" I asked.

"My husband, of course. Mr. G. P. Powell."

"You call him that?"

She nodded stiffly. "Yes. That's what he wants me to call him." She settled a little into her chair. "I'm a lucky woman and appreciate it. I never had anything and now I've got it all—anything I want. Cars, maids, clothes, sun time here and down south in Palm Beach. I've got credit cards and closets full of beautiful things . . ." Her voice died away without convincing either of us. It seemed to me that what I'd heard was taught, a voice repeating its goodies by learned rote, parroting what it had painfully been told too many times in too many places.

"You said Mr. Powell wasn't any help," I prompted her, when she remained silent.

"He'd had some drinks—just to relax," she said. "He wasn't feeling very good that day. We were all sitting there in our place in the big party room at Skid's, just sitting there, drinking. She got him drinks."

"Kate got drinks for Skid?"

"Yes. At the party. Like I said." She nodded, losing me, her eyes retreating to some never-never land.

96

"What happened then?"

She came back a little. "There were so many people around. I guess it was in his drink. I thought everything was going to be all right between them, but Skid fell down and started having real hard fits." She put her fingers up to her mouth and bit savagely at them. "Skid said out loud that she'd killed him." She leaned toward me. "She told me once she was going to kill him if he didn't leave her alone." She put her hand over her eyes. "But I didn't want to have testify to that about Kate." She took her hand away and looked at me. "They didn't make me testify."

"All right," I said soothingly, but she'd covered up again.

Her voice was so low I almost couldn't make it out. "Dr. Sam came in after a while, but it was too late for Skid." She shook her head and ran the hand away from her eyes. "They were all standing there and watching and Skid was having these fits on the floor and we knew, we knew . . ." She bent forward and the tears came. "He just died right there on the floor without anyone really helping him. And Kate was hysterical and she laughed and Mr. Powell hit at her with his cane, and . . ."

One of the Dobermans came easily up over the fence and toward me at a trot.

She said: "Down, Bowen. It's all right." The dog quivered under her hand and she shoved him back to the fence. He jumped over it reluctantly.

We heard a new sound together. The sliding door had opened.

A man came through the door, closing it behind him. He looked us over and nodded carefully at me.

He had a face that appeared to be carved out of old wood. He was a very big man, well over six feet, almost as tall as I was, thirty pounds heavier. His walk had a touch of uncertainty and I could smell old cigars and new bourbon upon him when he drew near.

She moved deep into her chair and I thought she was checking to make sure that nothing of her body showed so that we were suspect together. Far back in her eyes something ran and hid and I knew she was afraid of the man.

"This is my husband, Mr. Powell. This is Mr. Wright. He's Kate's new lawyer. Dave called and said we were supposed to talk to him."

"I know," he said. "But he was supposed to talk to me, not you."

He made no move to shake hands with me, as if that gesture wasn't necessary between us. He looked from his high place and saw me, but that was all. So I remained seated, nodding and smiling, watching both of them.

"Mr. Wright shouldn't bother you about it," he said chidingly, with a little less bluster. "You know how sick you got that night. The doctor's told you and told you that you weren't supposed to think about it anymore." He looked over at me, his eyes penetrating my own. "She loved Miss Kate before it happened and it would have hurt her to have to testify against her. That's why Mr. True didn't make her testify." He looked back at her. "Remember what Mr. True said? He didn't want you to get sick again. Remember what the doctor said?"

She nodded quickly. "I remember." She looked at me, her expression abject. "I was real sick for days after it happened." She turned back to him, her expression one of anxiousness, and he gave her a cursory little nod.

He turned to me again and smiled, exposing expensive-appearing bridgework. His hair seemed too full and I thought perhaps he was wearing a very good hairpiece.

"Maybe you'd like to go through my testimony again, Mr. Wright? I can remember it almost verbatim."

"I'd imagine you could," I said easily. "From your statement it would appear you were the first one to accuse Kate. Then it became a band wagon and everyone seemed to want to climb on."

He shrugged, not upset by my words. "There were lots of witnesses. That's why Susan here didn't have to testify. Mr. True said that her testimony was only . . . cumulative . . . I think the word was."

I waited, but he wasn't going to say anything more about that part of it. The silence grew.

He broke it. "Get me a bourbon and water, Susan." He laughed loudly, as if trying to show me he had a better, more congenial side than I'd witnessed. "It's dry as a desert outside." He looked me over shrewdly with small eyes, slits of brown in a less brown face. "What can she fix for you, son?"

"Bourbon and branch water will be fine," I said.

He nodded approvingly at me and Susie moved quickly away. Her lips seemed to be trembling a little and her body, when she discarded the towel, seemed slightly bent against the coldness he'd brought with him.

"Good woman," he said when she'd vanished. "But she is a nervous one. Doctor told me that she mustn't be bothered about what happened, that it upsets her, and that it could unbalance her. We didn't need her anyway. There were lots who saw what happened."

"I'm sorry if I upset her," I said, although I wasn't sorry.

He shook his head. "He said that one more good shock could put her over the edge. She eats those damned pills he gave her—those tranquillizers. Sooner or later she'll wind up in an institution," he said, and I thought the idea didn't completely displease him. He'd lived through a lot of troubles. Perhaps he now relished calamity, lived for discord. There are people like that.

"I hope things straighten out," I said.

He nodded.

"My father was supposed to see you," I said. "After the trial."

He shook his head. "I saw him in the Elks the afternoon before he died. But we didn't talk much."

"He didn't come out here then?"

"Not to my knowledge."

We waited.

"I understand you know my other son, Charles?" he said finally.

"We were in law school together," I said.

He nodded. "He thought you might be down after what happened to your father. Too bad about that." He measured me again with his eyes. "Some of these days we're going to have to get some good legal help at the plant. It'd maybe be part time for a while, perhaps a retainer sort of thing. Later, I imagine it would work into full time." He stopped and waited for me to say something.

I was saved for the moment by Susie Powell, who came bringing two bourbons and water and a cup of very black coffee. He took his and nodded at her. She handed mine to me without ever looking directly at me. Then she quickly left the room with the coffee.

I sipped at the drink and he took a good jolt from his. The bourbon seemed second rate, but there was a lot of it.

"Why not come talk to me about the job?" he said. "Perhaps something could work out. I'm sure you'd find us most generous."

"Thank you," I said noncommittally. "After this is over."

He laughed harshly. "There isn't much left. That woman killed my son. I fully intend to see that she pays for it one way or the other." He bent toward me, attempting I thought to bully me a little with his huge body. "She hated him, all right. I saw her out when Skid was gone away on trips. She always looked pretty happy when my boy wasn't around. That soldier boy was getting that, and maybe some others were too. I know women." He laughed without humor. "Been married enough times. That soldier was sneaking in. I told Skid that." He nodded briskly. "He believed it, too. She was just too slick for him to catch her in the act, but not too slick for us to know." He stopped and remembered it all and pain came into his eyes. "Then she poisoned him," he finished darkly.

"You saw her give him a drink that had poison in it?" I asked.

"That's right," he said. "I testified to that and to that soldier too on my oath. She gave it to him in his drink. Then she somehow got the glass and had it washed before the police got there—the glass that had the poison in it. She kept bringing him drinks all that evening, being sweet on the surface after they had that fight." He looked away from me. A pulse stirred rapidly at his temple. "I testified she was the only one who could have given it to him. And the jury believed it."

I smiled a little. "From what little I know about it, it seems to me a lot of people could have slipped something in his glass."

He shook his head. "She got his drinks from Johnathon. She got them all. She believed they'd all think it was just another heart attack. Good-looking woman wanting him to die, waiting for it, wanting my name and his name, the house and money. She'll never get anything if I have to burn in hell for it." He watched me with intent eyes that had looked over the rims of too many drinks in his long life. Things were no longer completely clear back of those eyes, but that didn't bother him. He was a man who'd decided and had no intention of being sane or reasonable about it. And he had great power. He'd shown that.

He waited for me to say something, and when I didn't say anything he nodded at me.

"A lot of witnesses testified about those drinks. If you want I'll give you their names."

"I know about them," I said. "Your employees, mostly."

"So what?"

I shrugged. "I've looked around some. I've got a likely candidate as an alternate. I thought maybe Johnathon Hartwick might have done it."

"The gardener?" He shook his head and grinned at me, some joke in mind that he wasn't going to share. "You can go down there to Bington if you want and try to talk to him." He turned away a little, pleased. "Smart, young lawyer like you—sure you can. He was passed out and now he's crazy."

I put down my glass.

Some realization came into his eyes that perhaps he'd been too hard, given too much of what he felt. "How about that job?" he asked. His voice was almost anxious.

"Maybe," I said, but I thought he read the answer in my eyes.

He stepped back one pace and nodded at me and I felt coldness run down my back, like tiny ice cubes falling into a glass. I felt as I'd felt when Anne Silver showed me the light bulb. Something I'd said, probably in turning down the job, had made him set his mind about me. He was wary for the first time, still wanting to get me on his side by whatever means it took, but now about to make a decision against me.

"I just want her punished," he said. "I told the governor that."

"I don't care what happens as long as she has a fair shake. I'll tell the governor that," I said.

"We're friends, you know."

I smiled. "Yes. I'd heard that." I looked into his old and merciless eyes. "A man needs his friends."

"Especially a man in politics," he said, gaining confidence.

"I may get out—stay here," I said, as if I was considering it. "I mean with your employment offer."

"On further thought, I don't think you'd be happy here," he said. "I know you wouldn't be happy here if you make more of a mess out of this thing. I thought Dave made that clear to you."

"I have to help my client," I said.

He looked up at me, calculating. I had a sudden inspiration. It seemed worth my time not to anger him any more, but leave him unsure as to what role I'd play. I owed him nothing. Especially not honesty.

I winked at him.

He watched me uncertainly.

"Don't worry so much about things," I said. "I know where I am and what I want to do." I turned away. "And thanks for the drink."

I left him there. I thought he was confused. The pretty black maid met me and escorted me to the door. When we were out of his sight she gave me a secret look and pressed a note into my hand. I pocketed it.

I waited until I was off the Powell place and down the road. There I pulled off to the side. I could see the lake, smell the wild flowers, and hear the bullfrogs grunting at the sun. My pulse was up a little.

The note was neatly printed in block letters. It read: "Come to 2315 Moses tonight at eight o'clock." It wasn't signed.

I drove the LTD to Pop's house and parked in his drive. The garage door was open and his car was parked inside. It was a ten-year-old Buick lovingly polished and with less than fifty thousand miles on it. I walked up his well-weeded walk and entered the silent house.

I wondered why he'd gotten into the case. If there'd been pressure brought to bear on me, then surely there'd been even more pressure brought on him. It was his town, the town he'd lived in all of his life. And G. P. Powell hadn't been interested in a trial—he'd wanted a modern lynching —nice and easy and just legal enough to satisfy a cursory glance. He'd wanted to buy me and someone, undoubtedly his daughter's husband, Dave Jordan, had told him I might be for sale. I imagined that now they might be even more encouraged about that.

And yet from what I'd seen and what I'd heard they'd had all of the evidence in the world.

Maybe Pop had found something. Maybe that was why . . .

I resolved to myself that I'd not dig around too much in that area of my mind on the evidence I now had. The light bulb wasn't that conclusive. Kids? An accidental happening? Maybe even the janitor himself trying to set up a hated employer?

But I couldn't get away from it that easily. Dave Jordan had put pressure on me because I could embarrass him in his corporate machinations. All he'd seemed interested in was time. And he'd paid me something for that time.

G.P. was an old and angry man.

I wondered why he was still angry.

And maybe if you can buy time you can also buy results.

The porch was cooler than outside in the sun. The yard was large, out of an easier time than the narrow-lotted tract houses of my day. Trees shaded the yard and porch.

I went out into the kitchen and found a glass and ran cold water and drank while I stared out into the yard. Perhaps, if I really tried, I could now find some permanence for myself here. It had been a long time since I'd stayed in other than a hotel. I thought again that the years with the bitter old women, the years of growing up, of seeing my mother waste away from lack of life and love, had made me skittish of continuing relationships. Wasn't it time to become a part of life? But I was a good time boy, a minor flash. I sat down at the kitchen table and wondered about myself and whether I had the bottom to really fight the good fight if they began seriously tampering with what I wanted. I wondered if I'd fold if they got to the governor. I remembered the girl in jail and hoped that I wouldn't. But I wasn't sure, not at all sure.

So be clever and careful.

The phone rang and startled me a little and I went down the hall and answered it.

"This is your friendly governor," a distinguished and known voice said. "What's going on down there? I keep getting calls."

"I'm going to have to stay," I said.

"I can certainly believe that," he said coolly. "You'd be surprised how many people down there are very interested in your welfare, people who want me to advise you on your possible courses of action." He stopped for a moment and then said: "What about the woman who killed her husband?"

"It's hard for me to sort things out, Governor. All I can say for now is that they seem to have had a lot of evidence against her and some of it might even be unpressured, unbought, spontaneous evidence. There appears to have been a little jury tampering at the trial and maybe some arm bending at the judicial stops. Other than for those minor things, everything seems to be just peachy keen."

"You don't sound happy about your present situation," he said. "I want you to know that my callers are much interested in what aid I can and will render you. So far I've been noncommittal. That's about as far as I can go for you unless you can show me some reason the governor's office ought to do more. You know I've got to and will treat you just as I'd treat anyone else." His voice sounded a bit defensive.

"I realize that, Governor. It's just that this seems to me to be a thing of family honor. And it also seems to me like there's a chance my father may have been pushed around a little."

"You mean like down some stairs?" he asked.

I hesitated. "Bad choice of words, I suppose," I said slowly.

"All right. No more. Keep in touch. I'll hold the job open up here a little while." He sounded a little wounded about my apparent desertion of post.

"Uh—can I ask you to check on something for me?"

"Maybe," he said unbendingly.

"There was an army captain who was stationed out at the plant. He was transferred right after the poisoning took place. His name was Joe Ringer. Can you check for me and see if anyone in the Powell family got him transferred, pressured a transfer for him. He's dead now. Got killed over in Asia. Get someone to try the normal sources on it—the district congressman and the two U.S. senators."

"Why do you need it?"

"He left in a hurry. They used him as the motive, or part of the motive, for the poisoning. Kate Powell was supposedly running with him and so she killed her husband. So I'd like to know who put the heat on for his transfer."

"I'll try." He stopped. "And you try to get along down there."

"Sure."

"You won't do it," he said.

"I'm trying," I insisted hollowly.

After we hung up I gave up further thought as a bad job and drove down to the Lichmont Hotel bar and got a tall drink and took it over and hid myself in a dark corner. Old apparitions came and bothered me. Once, long before, I'd brought dates here. Unlike the lake, the hotel hadn't updated things much from that faraway time. Then, it had been elegant. Now, it was fading away, done to slow death by bright chrome and plastic motel monstrosities that swarmed their rooms like summer bees near the four-lane edges of Lichmont.

I sat there and tried to remember just exactly why I'd left the town before, what had set me off. All I could remember were vague things. Maybe I'd decided Pop's values weren't mine. Sure, that was it, I made myself believe uneasily. I remembered: he would usually make his voice louder when talking long distance as if he was afraid that he couldn't be heard from city to city or state to state. I remembered he'd had some trite phrases that he constantly used so that each time I'd heard them then they had grated on me. The reasons I'd left seemed trivial now. But I had left.

I could see out the window. The sun was very low and a single evening cloud picketed it.

I remembered, for some reason, my time in war. That time seemed less real than the time I'd been in the town with Pop. All I could really remember was that a number of good people had died and I had lived. My trouble was that, even now, I couldn't agree with the selection process for living. I didn't then and couldn't now understand that you were supposed to do something because someone *said* it was good and right—like believing in words on paper called laws when those laws were misused; like seeing the good ones and the bad ones all mixed in the legislature so that what you got was a broth of unknown strength; like seeing a town like Lichmont responsive and responding to one man's wants. And I wasn't sure in my own mind that that man was sane. I wondered vaguely if anyone had any idea of how much alcohol had flowed in and flowed out.

I moved away and decided that really I'd left before for a couple of more cogent reasons. The first, as I remembered, was that I was "Young" Wright, considered trustworthy enough by Pop's clients to carry papers to the courthouse, but not good for much else. But another thing, even then, though there was no specific incident I could now remember, was the slight odor of decay to the town. Or maybe I'd just remembered that odor because of what I'd seen this day. I knew myself well enough to know that I can and do fantasy things to fit in with what I need at the moment.

I sat there in the faded bar and watched around me, deciding that nothing had really changed inside the place except that there was probably a new coat of dust under the secret places where morning sweepers couldn't reach. The only thing that had happened was that a few years had passed. And I was still me. And it seemed to me suddenly that the woman in jail was far more real to me than anyone I'd ever known or loved, father, mother, friends, governor, judges, and the rest.

But the woman in the jail couldn't be for me. I could help her if I wanted to help her and if I was cunning enough as a lawyer and could invent or find new truth—assuming that the truth wasn't something that would send her on to prison or to the electric chair, if they ever used it again. But I couldn't form any lasting relationship with her. I couldn't marry her for example. The party hierarchy wouldn't approve. I'd fail my political dental exam. I'd be dead as a candidate the first time someone reprinted her story and linked our names.

I wondered if I really gave a damn about going on, and decided that maybe I did. You always think you can change things. Politicians live on their ideals, even if they never get close to accomplishing them.

In a while I grew tired of chewing on myself and went into the dining room and got a sandwich. I lingered over that for a while, sitting near the window, watching the people pass by and renewing my acquaintance with General Ulysses S. Grant, who stood atop his raised stone and surveyed the park he'd commanded since I was a boy. The men in blue and gray were gone. So, someday my war would be a memory and a statue in a park across from an old, decaying motel.

2315 Moses was a two-story with cheap asphalt siding that tried hard to hide old scars. Two black children played in a bald tire swing in a front yard where the grass ran from sparse to nonexistent. I parked the LTD in front and resisted the urge to lock it. The oldest child, a boy, watched me climb out of the car. He stopped the swing.

"Mamma said for you just to wait out here," he said in a faraway voice, knowing me. "I'll tell her you're out here."

"Thank you," I said.

He vanished and the other child, a girl, turned her back on me and hummed to herself and kicked her heels against the parched ground.

"Would you want me to swing you?" I asked, intrigued. She shook her head too quickly and turned to look at me through black, black eyes. She was, I guessed, about eight or nine years old, perhaps two or three years younger than the boy who'd left to carry the message.

"Are you a policeman?" she asked curiously.

I shook my head.

"You can push me a little," she decided grudgingly.

I went over and got her going well enough so that she laughed in the wind.

After a time the black woman I'd seen at the Powell house earlier came onto her porch and watched us. The boy was with her. He pushed into my place at the swing and I went on up to the porch.

"I'm Mrs. Worthington and you can sit in that green lawn chair," she said. "I'll sit in the rocker. I got to be careful around here. Things can get nervous. I can't take you into the house and I can't meet you someplace else for fear someone sees me." She smiled with due care. "This town is up tight. Some pickets from this neighborhood went out to Mr. God P. Powell's plant and had a little march a few weeks back. I mean we don't get a fair percentage of the jobs out there." She shook her head. "You'd have thought we started a fight at the last supper. Someone went down and hired a bunch of badasses out of Louisville, I think, and they come sifting in here, black and white both. Some people got hurt, some houses got scorched and no one here trusts no one anymore." She gave me a cryptic look. "Maybe that's why I gave you the note. They got you sandbagged."

"Who has?"

"Them Powells. G.P. and his son-in-law at least. Maybe the daughter. Maybe even Miss Susie. I don't know about Charley. He don't come around so much."

"What can you tell me?"

"I can tell you they went over into another state and

hired a lawyer and flew him in here. He came out to the house a week or so before the trial and went through questions with some of the witnesses—like those who work at the plant. He got real rough with them, told them how they should act, cross-examined them. I heard a little of it." She shook her head. "They had a lot of witnesses. Not that they wasn't right."

I waited.

"You know old Walkin' Joe?"

"No."

"He was a real old man. Your daddy knew him. He used to walk his legs off night after night. It was like a sickness with him—that walking. Carry an old gunny sack over his shoulder with never nothin' in it and just walk and walk." She gave me a sidewise look to see if I was listening, and then went on, seeing that I was. "He was out that night that Mr. Skid died. He was right out there around the house. He didn't tell no one for fear they'd take it wrong and bother him around on it. Then he got sick and he told me."

"Why you?"

"Him and me was friends. Sometimes I'd feed him. When it was cold out I'd let him sleep on my back porch and be in out of the weather."

"Tell me what he saw at the Powell place?" I asked.

"It was Mr. Skid Powell's," she said. "That night."

I nodded.

"You know about Skid's place? You seen it?"

I shook my head. "Not yet."

"Up on the north side there's a woods, real nice bunch of trees. Walkin' Joe, he told me he stop there. Just to watch the lights, he say. He seen people running into the house and he watched. He told me he knew somethin' bad was goin' on. So he just stayed. After a while he seen a man and a woman come sneakin' out of the back way to the house. They washed something under the outside garden faucet and the man, he hugged her. Then they went back in. Joe watched for a while longer and then the fever come on him again and he had to walk so he starts off again. When he was a little away he heard the sirens comin' and he got afraid. Then, later, he heard about what had happened and he was real bad scared."

"Did he know the people?"

She shook her head. "Not him. But he tell me a little about them and I guessed who they were."

"All right. Who?"

She smiled crookedly. "Joe say the man's big and have on soldier's clothes—a officer's coat. Woman is tall and pretty." She nodded knowingly. "Guess who?"

"You think it was Kate and Captain Ringer."

She nodded solemnly. "I got a cousin works up in Georgeville twenty miles up the river. She used to see them come checking into her motel she worked at up there, Kate and her captain. Once she saw her come there with Charley, too." She shook her head, unwilling to comment on moralities. "But Skid was a mean one. Just like G.P. I don't blame Miss Kate. And I never said nothing."

"Charley," I mused.

She nodded.

"Did you tell my father anything at all before the trial?"

She shook her head. "I'm telling you because I heard how you talked to Mr. God P. this afternoon. I work for him, but I don't much like him."

"Telling me really doesn't help me much," I said gloomily.

She shrugged. It was enough for her that she'd given the information.

There was more than one soldier and more than one pretty woman. I remembered that.

"I want to talk to this old man."

She shook her head solemnly. "He's dead. Been dead for maybe two or three months now. Got to coughing in the spring. I tried my best to take care of him, got him a doctor and all, but he died." She nodded, remembering. "At the end his old legs was still moving in the bed. Doctor told me he had the legs of a young man." Her voice grew confidential. "No one knows about this. I don't even tell my Andy. Maybe it does something for you and maybe it doesn't. But I told you. Mr. God P. Powell ain't the end of all of it. Not for me, anyway."

The old man was dead. Even if I thought that he'd seen someone else other than Kate and her captain, it was too late for the evidence to do me any legal good. But I did know something that hadn't appeared in the trial. Maybe I could use it.

"It's evidence, ain't it?" she inquired.

"Sure it is," I said, but it wasn't.

She was pleased.

I found myself, curiously, jealous of Charley Powell.

"What did Susie Powell tell you to do when I came this afternoon?" I asked.

She watched me, her face expressionless.

"I came in and she told you to go do something."

She looked all around. "Call Mr. Powell," she whispered. She got up. "You better go on now. You been here long enough for insurance sellin' or whatever. My Andy comes home a bit after nine." She shivered visibly in the warm air, wary of the times. "Leave Miss Susie alone," she said. "She's a nice lady. She's sweet."

I shook my head. "I can't leave anyone alone. I may need to talk to you again."

I went back out through the yard when she turned away. The two black children played in the swing, both of them trying to pump it now. I got into the LTD and drove away.

I parked the car on the wide berm of the road along the river. There were other cars there, but they all seemed populated by couples, intent on other things.

Down below the river was at pool, moving slowly and easily toward its sea. Pleasure boats cut widening wake lines in the water. Two water skiers waved at each other.

The information that Mrs. Worthington had given me didn't really mean anything, but it had dropped my morale a little more, so that I was about as low as I could get. Yet it was something that Pop hadn't known, according to Mrs. Worthington. Another bit, another piece.

With the time available to me I'd have to stumble upon things or maybe the sheriff would have to stumble for me.

I sighed and leaned back in the seat to relax.

The police car pulled up ten yards in front of me. A uniformed officer got out. He walked regally back to my window. His smile was pleasant and businesslike.

"Why are you parked here, sir?"

"Watching the river," I said. "Like the others."

"I'll need to see your driver's license." He was still smiling.

I smiled back. It seemed a reasonable request. I had out-of-town plates. I got out my billfold and took out the license and handed it to him.

He read it carefully, then took the license with him and went to the rear of my car and began writing. I got out and he watched me expectantly, waiting, I believed, for me to protest.

A bald-headed man and his date/wife also watched cautiously from a car a few yards away. I walked over there while the officer continued writing.

"My name is Mike Wright," I said conversationally to the bald-headed man and his woman. "I'm an attorney here in town. I may need you to testify about what's happening here." I dug in my billfold and handed him a twenty-dollar bill. "Come past my office tomorrow and my secretary will make a statement out for you to sign."

He took the money, but he was reluctant.

"There'll be eighty bucks more if you get the names and/or license numbers of the other witnesses."

His lady crinkled the twenty from him and pursed it. She nodded at me. "We'll be there, mister."

The uniformed officer was watching. I'd kept my voice low, but he'd seen the twenty pass. I walked back up to him. His eyes were suspicious.

"You're parked too close to the street," he said, writing on his pad.

"Okay."

"You smell like you've been drinking, too. Good thing I didn't catch you driving."

"Would you like for me to start the car and drive it for you now?" I asked politely.

"You better leave it parked and take a cab where you have to go. We had a little girl killed by a drunk driver like you a few months back." His voice was now just a shade defensive.

"I'll be happy to drive it for you," I said. I opened the door.

"I told you not to drive," he said loudly. "I'm telling you again." He looked over at the bald-headed man's car. "You better move on there, mister."

The bald-headed man nodded quickly and started his car. He drove past us as the police officer waited, smiling again. But fifty yards up the street the car pulled in. I saw the woman get out of the car with a pencil in hand and approach the first car east of me. She ducked behind it and got the license number. She watched us.

"I'll move the car for you now, Officer."

He moved a step back. His collar seemed to have shrunk a little and he jerked at his shirt. "You've got a big mouth, Wright. Your daddy had one once too. You're pushing me and I'm going to make sure you pay for it."

I got in the car and turned the key and let the car inch forward a few feet and then reversed it back. I shut the motor off. His face had grown very red.

"You're going to jail for that," he said.

"Yes, sir." I waited for a minute. "You want to take me in your squad car or have me follow you. Or maybe you need to radio for help. I'll certainly oblige in any way I'm told." I raised my voice a little. "I now request that I be given a test at the local hospital for blood alcohol." I got out and raised my hands. "I suppose I am now under arrest."

"I'll tell you when you're under arrest."

I looked around again. I hadn't paid a lot of attention to the police car before, but I'd caught a tiny hint of movement when I got out.

"But you don't need assistance," I said. "You have help there in your police car. I wonder who that would be?"

"None of your damned business," he said desperately. "You get back in your car and move on away from here."

I walked on up to the squad car. Chief George Jett was sort of crouched into the front seat, his legs cramped, his face creased with lines.

"Hi there, Chief," I said friendlily.

In a low voice, inaudible five feet away, he gave me specific instructions about what I should do with myself and what parts of my anatomy and what parts of other people's

116

anatomy I should use in doing the job. It all sounded rather exciting, but probably impossible to accomplish.

"I am most impressed by your language and diction," I said in hopeless admiration when he was done.

The uniformed officer had moved up to stand behind me. I could hear him breathing heavily.

"Shall we take him on in, Chief?" he asked, his voice aching for it.

"Get in the car," the Chief said to him.

"I want him to see our back room," the officer said.

The little lady who'd been with the bald-headed man was still watching covertly.

"He gave that lady twenty dollars."

"Get in, I said," Chief Jett said. "I saw him."

"Okay, okay."

He got in and put the car in gear without looking back. They bounced out to the traveled portion of the street, throwing minor bits of gravel against my legs.

The lady who'd watched came back. "What was that all about?" she asked. "You weren't doing anything wrong."

"Oh yes," I said. "I was parked illegally. And I'm a known bad actor. I'm against money."

"Hunh?" she asked without comprehension.

"Thanks for the help," I said. "Don't forget to come past tomorrow."

"You really fixed them, didn't you?" she said in admiration. "And I helped." She was pleased about it.

"You sure helped," I said, and we parted friends.

I started the car again and drove down and away from the river and on out past the Powell plant. Its buildings sprawled, block on block, eating up a sizable part of the west end of town.

New buildings had been erected since the last time I'd

been in the area. Some of the buildings were protected by high fences, with barbed wire strands at the top. Armed, uniformed guards patrolled the fences. A few guards had leashed guard dogs as companions. I was watched with suspicion when I slowed my car. The guards appeared to be Army.

I parked in an area designated for that purpose and walked back to an opening in the fence. Two men in a guardhouse came out to meet me.

"My name is Mike Wright," I said to the one wearing sergeant's stripes. "I'm an attorney representing Mrs. Powell." I looked behind him at the buildings. "I'd like to take a look around in there."

He shook his head. "No one gets in this plant without a pass."

"Who would I see about obtaining a pass?"

"The commanding officer. But he'd have to go through some preliminaries on you." He shook his head. He was wearing Vietnam campaign and a Purple Heart ribbons. He seemed friendly enough. "People who want to go to work out here in this section normally have to wait a couple of weeks. I mean after they're accepted until they get clearance."

"I haven't got that much time," I said.

He shrugged indifferently. "Sorry about that."

"That would be Colonel Uhland?"

"Yes, sir."

"Do you have a telephone in your shack there?"

"Yes, sir."

"Would you please see if you can get him for me?"

He nodded and gestured to the other man, who was watching us carefully. "See if you can get Colonel Uhland for Mr. Wright," he ordered.

The other man dialed a four-digit number on the phone and listened for a while.

"No answer," he said.

"He's got an office down in the administration building, but he ain't around there much at nights," the sergeant explained. He waited, offering no further information.

"I'll catch him later on," I said. "What's so secret in there?"

He stiffened and lost his friendly attitude. "You'll have to ask him, sir."

"Do people who work for Powell come and go in here?"

"No, sir," he said. "This is a military reservation."

I nodded and walked back to the car. The two of them watched me carefully all of the way. As I went back past I thought they took my license number down.

I went restlessly to the office and read law for a while. Mostly I read poison cases. In Georgia a man was given some prussic acid, cyanide, by a loving wife. He walked seventeen steps (a prosecutor had counted them) down from his apartment to a store below, with the wife following him with avid interest. He fell and died without uttering a sound inside the store door. She was tried and convicted and the case was in the appeal records because of technical reasons.

In Kentucky a woman was killed by aconite and an appellate tribunal reversed the conviction of her supposed lover when it found too little evidence to sustain the verdict because of the sparsity of the testing done and the rather poor evidence that aconite had been the poison. I wrote the poison down in my memory in case I ever wanted to do away with someone. A judge, describing the poison, noted that in the Middle Ages it was punishable by death in some areas to possess the poison.

A woman described by unfriendly neighbors as a

"witch" in Illinois was tried and found guilty of poisoning an old man she'd cared for. She'd used arsenic in his enema over a period of weeks and, when death did not arrive fast enough to satisfy her, she'd given him large oral doses. Her conviction had been affirmed by the court, but there was a technical, dissenting opinion because of the witchcraft business and its effect on the home-town jury.

The last case Pop had on his list was of more than passing interest. In Indiana a man had been convicted of poisoning a rival for the affections of a woman, who had, unfortunately for the love-struck poisoner, been the wife of the deceased. The poison was strychnine, with some conflicting testimony indicating a possibility of brucine. On appeal the case had been reversed because there'd been no showing of evidence in the trial tracing possession of the drugs to the convicted man. In addition, the victim had eaten and drunk in several other places on the day of his death, and the appellate tribunal had expressed doubts about the proof as to when and where the poison had been administered. There had been medical evidence that death sometimes comes as quickly as a few minutes after a fatal dose—one-half grain or more normally—but sometimes the victim lingers on for a time, hours, days. I supposed Skid's heart condition might have hastened his demise, and reminded myself to seek further information from Dr. Sam Bush on that. But the case was a good one for me.

After that case Pop had done no more, other than Shepardizing, checking to see if cases had been overruled or modified. According to his notes, the Indiana case hadn't.

I sought and found a few more poison cases in the books. I read them all, with particular interest to those involving the vegetable poisons like strychnine. And so I read about pilocarpine, nicotine, the solanine group, ergot, atropine, locust, Ricinus, conium, digitalis, Oleander, etc.

At last, full to the brim with visited poison deaths, I gave it up for the night. I went out to my car and drove to Pop's house and went to bed in the room we had sometimes called mine. I slept lightly and that dream came to me where I was back in the jungle. It was a dream that was my own personal poison, and it was a well-known dream. The little men strapped me to a tree and did savage things to me. And I died. Only then did I manage to come awake.

I lay there in the unfamiliar bed with heart pounding while I tried to convince myself that all that remained was the dream of that bad time. Everything was still okay down there. A few times I'd had the dream when I'd been with a woman and it had rendered me temporarily impotent.

Outside I could hear the night sounds and I listened to them and there was something subtly wrong with them. Something was moving outside my window.

I lay there a while until I was sure and then I rolled softly off the bed, away from the window side of the room.

Whoever it was must have waited for a long time. He didn't bother now to try to break the window to the room. He cut loose with his shotgun through the window where I had been lying and then he shot once again in the same fashion so that I was deafened by the shotgun roar and the deadly swish of the pellets high above my head. The shots would not have hit me had I been in bed. I realized that.

I heard him moving away. Or maybe I heard *her* moving away. And I found that I was too frightened to go to the window to try to see what I could see. I excused myself for that by remembering it was dark and moonless outside. I just stayed where I was for a while. Shaking.

It didn't seem the thing to do to call the police. They might laugh. I called the sheriff. He wasn't in, but his deputy was.

In the morning, when Sheriff Alvie left me, after cheerily spending the night, I went to see Dr. Samuel Bush after calling and getting an early appointment.

My nerves were pretty much back together. People had tried to kill me before and all it had done then was scare the hell out of me. That was how it was now.

Alvie hadn't found anything of importance outside. No cigarette butts, no expended shells, no footprints.

"You got them on the run," he told me exultantly a couple of times. And nodded sagely. "Now you know."

My best desire was to drive the LTD back north at high speed.

War had made me a practicing coward.

But I really wondered about that flight of steps now. And I wondered about Kate Powell. What did I know that warranted my killing? I racked my brain about that. Mulling did no good. Not for now. It had probably only been a warning, done to frighten me away. Sure.

Dr. Bush had a new stylish clinic building in the luxurious northeast area of Lichmont. Around the clinic it was executive land. Fifty-thousand-dollar houses were commonplace. The clinic was erected to fit into the total picture of happy young Powell executives and their wives, with 2.3 children and 1.8 automobiles, color televisions, swimming pools, and shag rugs. The medical building was long and low with lots of glass. I parked in a spacious area adjoining it. Samuel Bush was one of three doctors named on an ornate bronze sign. I went on into the building and took a seat after giving my name to a young receptionist-nurse with pursed lips and a handsome, harried look. Around me people, in various stages of health, coughed, read magazines, stared into space, and/or discussed their ailments in fearsome detail with neighbors who waited impatiently to counter with their own symptoms. A few children played listlessly in a corner sandbox and I considered joining *them*.

After a bit my name was called and I was conducted to a small private office where I stood and waited longer, engrossing myself by reading Dr. Bush's various medical diplomas. He was, I found, certified to be a pathologist.

He came into the room with a brisk, practiced efficiency. He nodded at me, not remembering who I was or why I was here, and looked for my chart to read. I felt as if I should drop my pants and await the needle. Doctors don't really recognize most faces these days. They are more familiar with those areas they can and do attack with wonder hypos.

He was a medium-sized man, not large, not tiny. I smiled at him and he smiled back and I could see his professional teeth.

"I'm Mike Wright, Doctor. I talked to you about my father. Now I'm taking his place in the Kate Powell matter."

He nodded and sat down and drummed his fingers on his desk, waiting for my questions. He wasn't much older than me, but he was busier. I looked him over without envy, glad I was a lawyer, glad I wasn't a doctor.

"There isn't any more you can tell me about Pop?"

He shook his head. "You've heard it all."

I got out the bottle of pills and handed them to him. "Did you give him those?"

He looked at the bottle, took the top off and smelled, then shook a pill into his hand and examined.

"I guess I did," he said. "These are soda pills. He used them for stomach upset."

"Oh?"

He nodded sagely.

"Then we'll go on to Kate Powell."

He nodded again and waited.

"I understand you're also the county coroner?"

"Yes, I am."

"My list says you were at the party the night Skid died."

"I didn't get there until late. Kate and Skid were patients of mine. I was invited, but I had to go to the hospital early. I didn't get to the party until it was too late for Skid." He shook his head, remembering. "I tried heart massage and, earlier, mouth-to-mouth resuscitation, but he was dead. I got a little sick myself. Maybe that was from the mouth-to-mouth. It might just have been my own nerves. I won't say for sure. He'd vomited a little. I cleaned him up before I tried, but I could have gotten a little of it. I thought it was heart when I first checked him. He'd had a coronary a few years back. But then witnesses described the convulsions and I got a little curious." He looked up at me. "You know much about strychnine?"

I shook my head and lied. "Very little. I'm willing to learn more."

"I looked it up again before I testified at the trial. It's obtained from the seeds of a plant in the *strychnos* group. It's an alkaloid, as many of the more deadly vegetable poisons are. I'd say that someone administered Skid a hell of a jolt of it. Probably one of the sulfates. Enough to kill several men. If the dosage had been more subtle I might never have picked it up, but then it might not have killed him. Not that I identified it at the time, but the hard convulsions certainly weren't heart, and that's what was described to me. His face, in passage from life to death,

124

had a horrible grin. They call that grin *risus sardonicus*. There was froth at his mouth, the muscles of the abdomen and chest were in deep contraction. He was almost a classic strychnine case. I estimated he died within ten to fifteen minutes of the time the dose got into his system. I doubt that I could have saved him if I'd been on the scene and known what it was at the instant he began to exhibit symptoms of the poison." He shook his head.

"How do you think it was given to Skid?"

He shrugged. "In his drinks, I'd guess. I found nothing to make me believe otherwise."

"Did you find something to indicate that the poison *was* given to him in his drinks?"

"No. But there was other evidence than mine on how and when the poison was given him."

"Did you testify to any theory about where Kate Powell got the poison?"

"It's available. Especially around this town. Powell makes animal poisons. I was asked that."

"In a drink wouldn't he have tasted the strychnine?"

He nodded. "Probably. It's very bitter. But in a cola drink he could maybe swill it right down and not even know it except for a bitter aftertaste. Or the drink might have been so superloaded with it that one swallow could do the job, get enough into his system to kill him."

He stopped, but he wasn't done. I waited.

"They said he became very nervous and excited," he mused. "It starts out like that sometimes. It was over very soon. The convulsions were done by the time I got there and he was clinically dead. Maybe from the poison and maybe the hard convulsions just wore out his heart."

"Couldn't any of his symptoms have been caused by his heart condition?"

"Maybe," he said reasonably. "But not all of them. I do

believe the heart condition hurried his death. He had an attack a few years back, but it was just a warning. Slowed him down for a few months. As far as I was concerned his heart was sound again. It's probable that the attack made it easier for the drug to kill him."

"Was he taking anything for his heart condition?"

He shook his head. "All he took were vitamins. He was a nut on them. Thought they kept him virile." He grinned. "I guess he was virile enough."

"Did you yourself do any tests to identify the poison?"

He nodded. "I'm the coroner. We did an autopsy. I worked with the state police toxicologist. We did everything the books called for." He looked up at me. "Your father dug deep into that during the trial. But it was strychnine. Nothing else."

"What kind of tests did you do?"

"Removed some of the organs, tested the stomach contents. We worked with about two pints of contents we removed from the stomach. We found strychnine present. There was more than a grain of strychnine present for every ounce of contents. We also made what is known as a general analysis for poison and confirmed the other test. No other poisons found but strychnine. Enough of that to kill an individual like Skid, weight 230 pounds and fifty-five years of age. Much more than enough."

"How many of the symptoms Skid was supposed to have exhibited did you witness yourself?"

"Not a one. I only had them described to me. He was dead when I got there, as I said before."

"All right," I said. "Just exactly what did you see when you first came to the party and were called to attend Skid?"

He decided to humor me. "He was face down on the floor. His father said they'd turned him up a few minutes before but he turned back again just when he died in the last convulsion. Kate was standing there and so was old Mr. Powell, G.P. Then there was G.P.'s wife, Susie, and Geneva Jordan, his daughter. There were other people also, a crowd of people, but I forget who all was there." He looked up at me, trying valiantly for total recall. "I turned him over again and made a rather cursory, quick examination. He was dead. I didn't have my bag. It was in the car. I sent someone after it—Miss Susie, I think. I tried the massage and the other, but he was gone."

"Did you talk to Kate or did she talk to you?"

He shrugged. "Not really. In my opinion, and I certainly stated it—at the trial—she was in shock. I don't think her actions should have had much bearing on the question of her guilt or innocence."

"What actions?"

He looked away from me. "I told her he was gone. She laughed and cried all at the same time. Then she took my hand. I've heard it said that she's supposed to have shook it, but she didn't shake it. She only took it, the way a person in distress will do—seek closeness with another person. Then G.P. came after her with his cane and it was a messy scene. I gave Kate a sedative, made her take it actually. I had them put her to bed."

"How about G.P.?"

He smiled. "He didn't need anything. He'd had enough bourbon so that he wasn't tracking. He kept trying to shake Skid's body, rouse it. Except for that one moment when he went after Kate I don't think he really knew what had happened."

"Did you testify to that at the trial?"

He shook his head. "I was surprised. Your father never asked questions about it." He stopped. "He was pretty easy with me." He got a pack of cigarettes out of his pocket, expertly tapped one out, and looked longingly at it. "Trying to quit," he said, then lit the cigarette.

"Was Charles Powell at the party?" I asked curiously.

He nodded. "All of the family. Miss Susan, Geneva and her husband. I think Charles was the one who called the police." He looked at me. "That's a sick family, Mr. Wright. They hate each other a lot."

"Charles, too?"

He nodded. "He's probably the best of them," he admitted.

"How sick did the poison make you, assuming you did get some of it?"

"Not very sick. Just enough to further suspect what had happened to Skid Powell." He wet his lips, remembering.

I looked him over. "You're the first person I've talked to in this town who doesn't seem to have a lot of water to carry about what happened."

He looked back at me and his eyes were tired. "I work a fourteen-hour day, Mr. Wright. I've got a wife who's perpetually angry at me, children I seldom see, a house and a swimming pool and memberships I can't find time to enjoy. I frankly don't give a damn what keeps in this town. No one can pressure me and it's been tried I guess. By experts."

"How's that, Doctor?"

He grinned. "I got a call from Dave Jordan right before the trial. He wanted to know if I was still interested in doing physicals for the plant. The office made a peck of money on them last year. I wasn't sure, because Dave really didn't push it, but I got the idea I was being quizzed about how and to what I'd testify in the coming trial. When the physicals got interjected into the conversation I told him I really wasn't interested in doing them or in anything else. I mean, as far as the Powells are concerned."

128

He grinned at me again. "I can make a hell of a living in eight hours, Mr. Wright. And I can make it in other places than Lichmont if need be. But it never went that far. Dave even apologized. Said he didn't mean that the trial and the work we do here on physicals were connected." He nodded. "Maybe it was a coincidence, but I didn't think so." He looked at me. "I thought it was bad taste to get the two things mixed. Your father never asked me about that, either."

"You know they can and did pressure a lot of other people, don't you, Doctor?"

He nodded. "I guess I know it. Maybe because when the hospital needs something, when the town needs something, you don't go to the mayor or the county commissioners— you go to Dave Jordan; you go to G.P." He looked away from me. "And if you talk real nice you get it." His voice made allowances for them. "But it's their town. And the town's been good to me."

"Maybe anyplace would be," I said.

Prosecuting Attorney Jim True's office was spacious but drab. I gave my name to the first secretary interested enough to ask for it, and was told to wait. I sat in a rickety chair and watched the wall. Around me women of various ages argued and bickered among themselves about husbands who failed to pay support, eying me now and then with reflective anger, as if I was somehow responsible. I was a man and that was enough for them.

We have built a whole class of women like them, and we increase the numbers daily. Millions of them. When the support is set too high, when the male foot itches for a warmer place, then the man moves on. Prosecutors cannot prosecute unless they can find. Many States attorneys wink at men who are delinquent on support. The law is an impossible hodgepodge, not really made to punish, but to help enforce support. There are criminal penalties, but the man who returns to again help shoulder the load is normally given a slap on the wrist and a wink of the male eye.

And so the women live on hope and welfare. I once knew one who legitimately had six children by four different fathers. Someone was always behind on support and she lived from crisis to crisis. Keeping track of her various support payments was a never-ending job for the court's clerk.

But no one starves, they say. As if that was an answer.

If you think about it you can see possible answers. Make federal laws that enforce support and set that support on both need and ability to pay. Set up a situation where social security easily divulges information about employment, so that the wanderer can be traced. Take away the escape.

But it won't happen that easily. We live in a land that resists change, that guards its inequities jealously. Few lobby for the deserted. And more money through the welfare departments means more power and more people in the welfare departments. To tamper is un-American.

After a while the secretary beckoned me and I was called ahead out of order. I left the women huddled in unreasoning anger behind me. The secretary led me down a shabbily carpeted hall to a large inner office. Inside it friend Jim True shook my hand carefully and sat me down on another hard chair.

"I hear bad things keep happening to you," he said. "Like shotguns."

I nodded. "I guess it was done to frighten me. Whoever it was fired both shots way above my head. I figured that if I was supposed to get shot he'd have sprayed things closer around in the general area he thought I was in. Not that I was in it."

"You see anything?"

"I was on the floor," I admitted. "It seemed like a good place."

He smiled and offered me a cigar.

"You can smoke it," he said enviously. "I'll chew mine and breathe in the smoke. Doctor's orders."

I shook my head and he put the spare cigar regretfully back in his pocket.

"Chief of police was in earlier also. Something about you being disrespectful to one of his officers last night." He watched me, his face without expression.

"If he has any charges he'd like to file about that, then I'm available," I said. "I'm sure he knows that."

He shook his head. "He didn't say anything about filing charges. It was just mentioned in a regular visit. He comes in two or three times a week so that we don't get things too messed up between us. That isn't easy."

I nodded and lost interest. The chief of police was a symptom and not the disease.

"Tell me about the Powells and the trial. How much pressure did they put on you?"

"Some. But the case was good. I had eyeball witnesses that G.P. sent in here to me. They came through good. I had enough stuff for overkill in the trial. And maybe your dad wasn't too well at that. He wasn't at his best. I got some things in I normally might not have managed and his cross-examinations seemed halfhearted at times." He shook his head. "If you take an appeal up your job may not be a very palatable one. You may have to pick at your own father. You'd probably be better off to hire her one of those national hotshots. It can hurt you around here and in the state to get into one of these things, even as late as you're in. You'd have to fight the Powells. They're tricky.

Your father must have had a lot of second thoughts about being in it." He nodded. "Maybe . . ."

"Maybe what?" I asked.

"Nothing, I guess. It's just that I try to run my office. Now and then it gets away from me. Kate Powell was one of those times. I didn't like it being that way. Gift horse."

I said: "The Powells hired a lawyer to come in from out of town. It's legal to do it, I suppose. I hear he helped them get together on the stories. Made for smooth telling in a courtroom. Lawyer can help you gloss over anything that doesn't sound right."

He gave me a funny look. "I swear I didn't know."

"If I find anything at all can I come to you?" I asked.

"There isn't anything," he said carefully.

"All right," I said.

"I'd maybe talk about it." He shook his head apologetically. "This one is over. She gets sentenced Monday. I had her dead in my sights in court. Your dad knew that. What could there be?"

"I'll admit there really isn't anything so far. Nothing concrete. I just find it tough to trust all of that money. And I find it hard to trust shotgun blasts through Pop's windows or your local finest trying to put the roust on me." I looked at him. "Someone had to tell them to do that, Jim. And I don't believe your city administration is capable of such an original thought."

He gave me a smile. "I hear more about things than I normally let on. I've got a few good ones down there at City Hall. Enough around to keep me in touch with what's going on. I got a call about what happened to you with the Chief. And I found out early this morning about the shotgun blasts." He shook his head. "What you've got to understand is that you're involved in an unpopular cause, Mike. Your dad had problems and you've inherited them.

That could be most of it. But I do wonder about the shotgun. As to the city, they run their own little municipal empire down there. I never go to city court. That's where they'd originally take you. I doubt you'd be very welcome. If the Chief didn't like you, you can be sure the city judge would feel just exactly the same." He grinned. "But Powell runs this town. I just hold an office in it."

"What if I'd show to you that you've been used?"

He shook his head. "I don't think you can."

He sat there, smiling, and I went over it again in my mind. I really didn't have much.

"I just don't think this town should operate the way it does operate."

"You're right, of course. But the town believes that what's good for Powell is good for Lichmont. Right now getting Kate Powell sentenced appears to be the big thing." He eyed me. "You know they offered to hire me some big time help for the trial?"

"No, but I guess that's maybe the reason I want someplace to run to if things get any screwier." I looked at him. "What would it mean to you if the rest of this thing didn't go their way?"

He shrugged. "A lot of chest beating. Some publicity in their newspaper. I wouldn't like it, but I could live with it." He nodded, appraising me. "I guess I'd maybe listen if you really get something, but I can't believe there is anything. You want to tell me anymore now?"

"Nope. There isn't that much to tell."

"I thought G.P. might be satisfied with a plea of guilty to second degree. It's a life sentence, but she'd have been eligible for parole in six or eight years." He sighed. "I merely tell you about it because I made that proposition to your dad without recommendation. I think G.P. was reluctant to have his family messes trumpeted in court and in the newspapers. Maybe you could trade an appeal for it now."

"No chance," I said. "She says she's innocent, Jim."

"Sure. No chance of the death penalty if she takes it, though. Not that anyone has it happen, in fact."

"G.P. would inherit the estate if she made that deal. You know that he does inherit most of it if the verdict of guilty stands up?"

"I'd thought about it, but not hard. He has so much now. Why would he need more?"

"You always need more."

He nodded. "True, I guess."

"Looking around, you seem to have a lot of hot stuff going on in your town, Mr. Prosecutor," I said.

He flushed a little but didn't get angry. "I prosecute what they bring me. I call a grand jury now and then when the paper gets hopped up about sin. Some of the rough places shut down for a while. They always open up again. Old G.P. likes a live town. Helps keep union trouble away, he says. Keeps his workers happy. I've got a police chief who agrees with him. I start digging a finger in and things seem to go bad. My appropriations don't get through the county council, and I can't hire any help. So I let live and wait."

"All right," I said.

"You'll be there with her Monday?" he asked.

I nodded. "I suppose."

"About the town," he said. "The town's bad out there in my waiting room, too. It's a thousand women whose husbands can't or won't support the kids. It's thieves and con men and burglars." He shook his head. "I spend fourteen hours a day at this job and it isn't enough." He hesitated and I thought he was going to stop, but he went on, looking away from me. "I'm a reasonable man, Mike. I don't much like being part of the furniture. You keep in touch, hear?"

I nodded and felt a little better. Not brighter, but better.

In the office my witness of last night had not yet appeared. I picked up Anne Silver and we left a time of return note on the door.

I drove out to Skid Powell's house. She directed the way.

I thought about my interview with Jim True as I was driving. What he'd said didn't mean much. But I felt better about having an ear that just might listen.

Skid Powell's house had a big swimming pool in the front room, which really impressed me. I'd never seen a swimming pool in the front room of a house before and I'd fooled with politicians, many of whom will blow the whole bundle to make an impression.

The pool was now as empty as an August creek.

A guard stopped us at the front gate and let us in only after making several telephone calls. The guard was a big man with a heavy growth of beard. All of the time he made the calls he fingered his holstered revolver. His hands were as dirty as a pile of old snow.

"I don't like guns," Anne Silver told me in a whisper.

Finally the guard grudgingly told us we could go in and admonished us about removing anything, still fingering.

The "party" room was behind the pool. It was a huge family room, easily fifty feet long by about thirty or so wide. Ornate couches were arranged here and there into what polite society terms conversation groups. There were two big stone fireplaces, one at each end of the room. Above the northern fireplace an artist had caught a younger G. P. Powell in a stern pose, his eyes aloof. At the other end there was a picture of Kate Powell, a full length portrait. The artist had captured some of her vitality and beauty, but he'd missed on her eyes. In the picture they were serene and somehow waiting. I stopped and stared at her picture for a long time feeling desire within me.

Anne Silver tugged at my arm and brought me back to myself. She pointed.

"See how those two bay windows are almost large enough to be called rooms by themselves?"

She was right. They were huge. Double window doors opened out from them onto a stone patio.

"The way it was explained to your father and me was that G.P. and Kate and Skid and, sometimes, Miss Susie and Charley and Geneva sat most of the evening in the first bay window area. G.P. held court there. I mean he'd get up and wander around and talk to people now and then, I guess, and so would the others, but this was kind of their permanent place." She led me into it. There was a couch with a small table at each end and there were three chairs at intervals around the couch.

"Most of the time Kate and Skid were sitting on the north side of the couch. He was next to the arm. G.P. was sitting in the biggest of the chairs there, the nearest one to Skid. Geneva Jordan had another chair and Susie the last, but they weren't around much. They were all up and down, drinking, talking. Susie was pushing at people for a charity she was working on—something about trying to get a symphony orchestra to come here to Lichmont to play for us poor savages. The others who were here were mostly from the plant, plus the mayor and a few townspeople. There's a list in the file. Your father and the sheriff checked them all out and got no help."

I nodded and looked all around the room. The ceiling was high and beamed with beautiful slabs of dark and massive wood. The furniture was lovely, but all of it taken together had a curiously sterile effect—as if someone had put the whole thing together for parties and now, without one, it had died.

I left Anne and walked on up to the double window doors. The curtains were thin enough to see through, rich enough to filter the sun. Beyond the patio I could see the yard. A hose was attached to a water tap near the window and a sprinkler turned slowly in the middle of a still-cared-for lawn.

"Who stays here now?" I asked.

"I don't think anyone does." She joined me in staring out the window. "I guess Mr. Powell sends his people over here to take care of it. They say he won't come here himself now. I suppose he figures someone has to do it. The pool had water in it when your father and I were here." She pointed at the couch. "Skid fell right there in front of that sofa. He never got up again."

"Where's the kitchen where the drinks were being made?"

She pointed to the left. "Through that door." She shook her head, puzzled at my interest.

I said: "Any one of the others could have done it. A lot of people could have. It's been glued together that it's Kate." I shook my head.

"You have to prove it was someone else. Too late for that."

"I suppose," I said, and nodded. "Will you wait here for me? I want to look around upstairs."

"All right."

I looked around at the big party room one more time and tried to fix it in my memory. In the harshness of the daylight it was difficult to believe that a man had been killed here.

Or had he even been killed?

I remembered the things that people had told me, the

137

things I'd seen, and I felt a tiny drop of perspiration start down my back.

I shook my head to clear it. Suicide with an attempt at placing suspicion on Kate would be hard for Jim True to buy.

That didn't mean it wasn't something I should consider trying to sell.

I went on upstairs, but everything personal had been stripped clean. There was nothing in any of the rooms that gave any hint about the lives of those who'd once inhabited the house.

Charley Powell picked me up at eight that night. He brought along a pair of rather memorable-looking girls, as he'd halfway promised. His was tawny-haired, with easy eyes, a laugh that came pretty often, and an astonishing development between neck and waist. Mine was a smaller girl with very dark hair and a lovely, child-woman body. As soon as we met she took my hand in hers and held it feverishly. While she talked to me she watched Charley all of the time. She had sharp little teeth and she was extremely nervous, picking all of the time with her free hand at invisible pieces of lint on her dress and my best suit.

Her name was Fern plus something long and Polish. Charley's *other* girl, the one he was with for the evening, was named Rosa.

Fern and I sat in the back seat of the Lincoln and I tried gracefully to extricate my hand. When I'd get the job done, she'd manage to clasp it again before I could hide it away. Maybe it was a protective movement.

Charley said: "This town's kind of sad to travel. There are a few places that are okay, but not special. There's the Elks and the country club if you insist." He nodded at me, relishing something. "But I'm going to put you on my boat and take you upriver unless you disapprove. So you just lean back and get to know Miss Fern there."

He drove carefully down a side street toward the river.

Fern said: "I'm not married. Are you married?"

"Not me," I said.

She watched the front seat, where Rosa was hanging onto Charley tightly.

"Charley said you weren't, but I like to get my own answers. How long have you known Charley?" she asked me in a voice that thinned as she watched Rosa.

"I knew him in law school."

She nodded. "That's right. He said you were a lawyer. You're some kind of relation to that Mr. Wright that had an office down by the courthouse, ain't you?"

"He was my father."

"I knew him," she said. "He got my divorce for me— got me custody of my kid and everything."

"You've got a child?" I asked, attempting amazement.

"Sure," she said proudly. "She's almost four now. A little lady." She shook her head ruefully. "I got married when I was like seventeen. My folks tried to talk me out of it. They were right, I guess, but who admits parents are right at seventeen? My husband wasn't anybody from here. He was from across the river. It didn't last too long. All he was interested in was his car and combing his hair after he got me pregnant." She laughed carefully. "That's all he's interested in now, from what I hear." She looked at Charley's back with Rosa's arm possessively around it and pursed her lips and looked back to me. "Your dad was going to get him in court for me once. He's way behind on his support. Maybe you could do that for me?"

I nodded vaguely. "Maybe, sometime."

Her eyes opened wider, as if she'd discovered something.

"Hey, you're *her* lawyer. Kate Powell's. I wouldn't have thought you and Charley . . ."

"Charley's been fair," I said shortly.

In the front seat Charley braked and we parked in a graveled lot. A vagrant wind brought up the smell of the river. A walkway led down to a marina where scores of boats were tied to moorings. Voices called too loudly at each other and there were impromptu parties going on on several boats. Charley was hailed several times but moved on purposefully, waving a negligent hand at the greeters. The girls and I sailed behind him, riding in his wake.

The boat was named *First Fling*. It was about forty feet of swank cabin cruiser. Charley turned on the blowers and went below and fixed drinks while the girls got out cushions and deck chairs with a familiarity which indicated other visits.

I untied and Charley got us out in the river. The twin motors ran sweetly. Rosa piloted. Charley directed.

Fern sat down next to me and took my hand.

"Do you know Kate?" I asked.

"Not really. I've seen her around a few times. She's beautiful." Her eyes seemed green in the reflected light from the open cabin door. "She can sure wear clothes for an older lady."

I smiled to myself. Kate was maybe eight or nine years older than Fern if my calculations were right. These days that can be almost a lifetime.

"I knew Skid, though," she said. "I worked out in the plant for a while in the secretarial pool. I got to know Skid. We had a few laughs once or twice. I met Charley through him."

"Was Skid taking you out after he was married to Kate?"

"I guess so," she said, surprised at the question. "I guess

you'd call them dates. He'd want me to meet him someplace or other and I'd get in my Volks and buzz over. It wasn't anything serious." She shook her head. "He was a peculiar guy. Once I was out with someone else—a boy I knew—and we ran into him. Skid got real mad when he saw me with someone else—and him a married man and all. For a while I thought there was going to be trouble, but this Bill, the boy I was with, is from across the river too and he's pretty big and tough and nobody much tries to push him around. Skid was mad, but he wasn't stupid." She nodded, relishing the thought. "I wish he'd caught me with my ex-husband. He isn't very big or very tough. Maybe Skid would have knocked him around a little, pulled some of his pretty hair out."

"Maybe he would have at that." I watched her for a moment, thinking. "Would you be willing to sign an affidavit that you went out with him a few times?"

She shook her head quickly. "Not me. I've got my little girl to think about. I do that and maybe my ex hears about it and tries to take my baby from me."

"He wouldn't get very far," I said. "He'd have to prove you're an unfit mother. A few drinks and a few laughs won't accomplish that for him."

"Skid was married," she protested darkly.

I smiled at her. "That doesn't make much difference."

Charley turned from where he was watching Rosa pilot. I'd thought our voices were low, but he'd heard them.

"If Mike wants you to do that for him, Fern, then you ought to do it."

"For her?" she asked, surprised.

He nodded, his back toward us again. His voice was very low, but I heard it. "Maybe for me, too."

She looked us both over, her eyes not comprehending. "Okay, crazies," she said dubiously. "But if my ex even tries to take my kid both you lawyers are going to have to defend me. I'm not losing my kid for no one."

I gave her my most confident look. "We'll protect you. And with what you said about him being busy with his car and his hair he wouldn't have any time for a kid anyhow."

She smiled a little at that, but she still was dubious.

Charley took the wheel and piloted the boat up a side stream, reducing speed, flashing his spotlight. Both sides of the stream were guarded by fencing, most of it barbed wire, overgrown now with red roses, acres and acres of them. As the boat slipped up the strip of water I had the feeling that we were moving through a parted river of blood. Signs warned of grave penalties for trespassers.

We soon came to a huge old house, colonial in style, fronted by five porch pillars. Discreet lights outlined it. There was a long dock in front and it was guarded by a man in uniform. A large number of other boats were tied there.

"Private police," Charley said surreptitiously. He smiled at the man.

The man smiled back and touched his cap. "Evenin', Mr. Powell," he said. "Throw me the line."

"Hi, Harlan."

"I'll ask you to let me tie it, please. There's a pretty fair crowd tonight. I may have to move you around. Will you and your friends be staying for dinner?"

"I believe so," Charley said.

"I'll phone ahead and tell them there are four of you," the guard said.

"This place used to belong to David Vance," Fern whispered softly to me, taking my hand again as we started up a long walk. "Remember him? He was in the movies. He came here with maybe his sixth wife and built the house. Then he went bankrupt and the government sold house and land at auction for taxes. The Powells bought it and the land on both sides as a club for their executive people." She nodded out into the darkness. "There's an eighteen-hole golf course on top of the hill that way. On the other side of the house there's a swimming pool and some tennis courts. You can get here by road, but a lot of people come by boat."

We went through an impressive door into the entrance hall. Off to the right there was an intimate sort of bar. Stag men dressed in dark coats and white shoes, seated along the bar, appraised Charley's girls appreciatively from their vantage point while they argued golf scores. Along all the walls there were lines of slot machines, the old kind with pull-down handles, not the newer more sophisticated, electronic no-armed bandits.

A waspish appearing man of middle years approached wearing a dinner jacket and an air of authority.

"Hello, Mr. Powell," he said easily. "Nice to have you with us tonight. It's been a while. Perhaps tonight is family reunion night." He shook hands with Charley and nodded at me, not really knowing who I was, but willing to accept Charley as my credential. Then he turned and led us into the dining room. He seated Charley's girls around a table with enough dining implements for a half-day orgy, plus snowy white linens and burning candles. Around us other diners, similarly fitted out, ate discreetly and made muted sounds of polite conversation. Eyes considered us. Many seemed hostile.

Loudly enough for any straining listener to hear, Charley said to the man in the dinner jacket: "This is Mike Wright. I'll want you to make up a guest card for him. Perhaps he'll want to use the place again while he's in Lichmont." He turned to me and lifted one eyebrow, admiring his own performance. "Mike, meet Duane Geiger, our manager."

Heads turned to watch more closely. I felt as if I was being checked to see if my deodorant had faded. In a world where inventing a new name for a hamburger can make a man a quick million, lawyers involved with persons convicted of crime really don't rate very high in the pecking order. Especially in the opposition's club.

"All in the family, you know," Charley said, smiling. "He represents my sister-in-law now."

Mr. Geiger bent over and whispered something to him.

Charley looked at me. "Father is dining on the terrace," he said, and smiled. "With the colonel and Judge Stickney."

I nodded.

Mr. Geiger scuttled away.

A pert waitress in a cocktail dress took our dinner order. The girls excused themselves and went someplace with the announced purpose of painting and powdering. Charley looked me over grinning.

"By now they know you're here," he said. "But just to make sure let's sneak out to the bar for a quick one. One of G.P.'s toadies will surely be out there and will let them know."

"Why do you want them to know?" I asked.

"I have my reasons," he grinned. "I'm sure you'll discover them as time goes on, if you don't already know."

"I'm with you," I said agreeably.

"To the bar, then. By the time we get back they should have some drinking ammunition on the table and from out there we can see the girls come back down from their dream room—if they should by chance make it before we finish our drinks." He got up and punched me lightly on the arm. "What do you think of your little doll?"

144

"Very ornamental."

"I thought you might find her of special value. I mean she's friendly and then she was close to the family and all." He smiled with measured malice and led me toward the bar. I wondered some more about him.

Several hailed him from the bar. We got our drinks and he introduced me around, emphasizing the fact that I was representing Kate. When he did that it seemed to me that the crowd thinned quickly.

"Mike's an old buddy from law school," he explained. He drank his drink like medicine and ordered another. "Got to take care of old buddies—visiting bar men." He smiled at his own pun and patted me on the back. Then, before anything could happen or anyone engage us in conversation, he led me quickly back out of the small stag bar and to our table.

"That, my boy, will spread the red-eyed word," he said.

"Tell me why you want it spread?" I asked, guessing.

"For your sake and more my sake," he said. "I think you know where you are, Mike. This is my father's town. I could tell you a hundred stories about people who've gone up against him and wound up losers. Your father wasn't the first. Right now G.P. wants things to happen to Kate, bad things. He's used his tame police force and his well-schooled witnesses to make certain of it. A lot of people who testified in Kate's case weren't testifying to what they actually saw, but what he *told* them they saw. Rigging was the game." He nodded. "And when you start looking over the list of good and true jurors just remember that he saw that list too. More than half of that panel, one way or another, was connected to the plant, by working there, by marriage, by child, parent. The rest all knew about the plant. Your dad knew the risk. We talked about it. And

145

it's still that way for you. So right now if one Powell appears to be on your side it can at least confuse things."

I nodded.

He continued: "And there may be a value for me. If you get a reversal on appeal then Kate gets her half of Skid's stock. Even if it can't be voted for me this time then maybe she can vote it my way some future year."

I'd already pretty much figured it out, but I feigned surprise. "You're in with the ones trying to take over?" I snapped my fingers, trying to remember the name. "Medical Consultants?"

He smiled at me and looked around the room and lowered his voice. "I wouldn't be upset if they won out. We could move the plant up into the twentieth century."

"And beat your father?" I added.

He shrugged. "You've still got a lot to learn about the Powell family, Mike."

"I'll admit that," I said.

He shook his head. "Someday I'll run that plant, Mike. I've got a father who suffers from acute, alcoholic senility and who gave what should be my job to a man who hasn't got it and never will have it as far as managing is concerned. Powell will die with Dave Jordan running things. He thinks that you can get all your answers from computers. Computers are useful things, but only when men interpret them." He leaned back in his chair so that his eyes were shadowed. I thought he was slightly drunk. "I try to act like I don't care and that it doesn't make any difference to me. But it does make a difference."

"I'd help if I knew how," I said.

He smiled. "All you've got to do is get Kate out of trouble and talk her into changing her mind about me. So the stock would be voted for my people."

"Sounds easy," I said sarcastically. "Is she angry at you?"

146

"I made a mistake with her once. I tried to put the make on. Things got very cool." He looked away. "I was drinking. It seemed like a good idea at the time."

My heart leaped. "Did you take her to a motel up the river? In Georgeville?"

He nodded. "I said I just wanted to talk." He gave me a careful look. What I had said had sobered him. "How did you know about it?"

"I'm finding out a few things," I said.

He smiled. "Keep digging. The plant was buzzing today. I heard the governor was going to send the state police in, I heard that the charges were going to be dismissed, I heard you were secretly tied in with the unions and/or the Mafia." He shook his head ruefully. "You've got them nervous at least."

"Tell me more about your father?"

"What's to tell?"

"Anything you can think of."

He shook his head slowly and looked back in his past. "He sent me away. My family life has been a series of departures. First there was prep school. My mother died when I was in prep school. I was allowed home for five days then. It was my longest visit for a long time, before and after. There was Culver Military or a summer camp for vacations. Later, there was college." He looked at me, his eyes bitter. "I hated him then and I haven't changed. I think he sent me to schools and hoped I'd flunk out of them. The idea was to keep me busy, out of trouble, and away. Mostly away. My mother had left her stock in the company in trust for me with the bank. It's his bank. He manipulates it like he does everything else. Right before I turned twenty-one he talked the bank into getting an order to sell it, then tried to buy it through a third party sale. I had to hire a lawyer to get that stopped." He shook his

147

head again, this time in rueful admiration. "He's an old pirate, Mike. He's run this town his own way for fifty years and he's got no intention of letting anyone thwart him. Right now there's the stock. He'd like to be able to vote it all, but if that can't happen, then Kate can't be allowed to vote hers because we're after his butt end like a mad bulldog. If he gets the murder case finished successfully, then he inherits Kate's shares as the nearest relative. Then he can vote all the stock that would have been Kate's. It's close now."

"He tried to hire me," I said.

He did a double take. "That I hadn't heard, not even in plant rumors. But it would be a good investment for him. No matter what you charged it would be cheap compared to what's at stake." He gave me an intent look. "Do you know what Skid's stock is worth?"

I shook my head.

He computed idly with a fork on the tablecloth. "He had maybe a little more than twice what I've got. Let's say a minimum of fifteen and a maximum of eighteen."

I waited, afraid to ask.

"Million," he finished.

"My lord," I said, impressed.

"That's at the going price now and there isn't any available at that price. If it were all dumped into the over-the-counter market at one time it maybe wouldn't bring the top figure, but it would bring at least the fifteen."

"I see. And under the will Kate would have gotten half?"

He nodded. "I could win with that half. Handily. They've got the rest of the family tied up. G.P. will leave me nothing. I know that. Everything goes to Geneva when he dies."

"He left you out, then?"

148

He nodded. The faraway look came into his eyes. His voice was bitter. "He—he has more than Skid did," he said, refusing to say his father's name. "My half sister doesn't have very much now." He nodded at me. "I could sell mine out and wind up, after taxes, with maybe about seven million. I could buy myself some municipals, have an income in six figures and no taxes to worry with. And that kind of money will buy about anything, Mike. But I can't do that. I feel like I was born to run the plant, that my children, when I have them someday, should run the plant. I'm the only Powell who's left who can have kids. I don't want to sit down in Florida or Acapulco vegetating on the boat, playing bad golf for my kicks, and drinking myself to death. I want to work in the business. Somehow the law thing's gotten away from me. I guess I'm glad I went to law school, but the business is all that's left."

"I hope it works out for you," I said, finding it hard to be sorry about seven million dollars.

He shook his head. "He's always won. Maybe all I'm doing is driving up my buy-out value by being a nuisance."

The girls came back. I was happy to see them. Charley in the seven million dumps wasn't my idea of a pleasant way to spend the evening.

He brightened as the evening went on, but he kept watching the door to the terrace. Other people came and went, but not G. P. Powell. Other areas were crowded, but around us there were vacant tables. Bad weather coming. The food was fine and the waitress was attentive. I drank Heineken's beer, which has a real kick to it, and tried to get around a succulent steak. When the meal was almost done the lights went down as someone lowered the rheostat and a combo took over the far end of the room and began to play soft music. There were three of them and they had a little sign they put up that announced they were the "Availables." They were pretty good, piano, sax, and bass.

A man and a woman came in and occupied a table not too far away and I recognized the man. It was Dave Jordan and I nudged Charley, but he'd seen them also.

"I'd like to meet your half sister, Geneva Jordan," I said.

He nodded. "I'll take you over. At this time of night I wouldn't expect too much from her."

"How's that?" I asked, knowing.

He shrugged the question off and we made excuses to the girls and threaded our way between tables to where Dave Jordan and his wife sat. He saw us coming and I thought he whispered something to the woman, but I wasn't sure in the dim light.

Charley's manner was formal. "This is my sister, Geneva," he said. "You've already met Dave." He nodded. "And this is Mike Wright, Geneva."

"Sit down," Dave said carefully. "Please sit down."

Geneva nodded. Her eyes were strange. They seemed to focus on me with difficulty.

"I've got to get back to the table and patrol our girls," Charley said.

She nodded vaguely. "I see you do have a couple of your little secretarial types out."

He grinned at her, nodded at me, and was gone.

I sat down and inspected her further. It seemed to me that she was without either beauty or ugliness. Something in her life had soured her and that sourness was what you saw. I thought she was probably in her late thirties or early forties. Her hair and dress were fashionable, but the dress hung a little, as if she'd been heavier when she bought it. There were deep frown lines around her thin mouth.

"Would you both like a drink?" Dave asked.

"No," she said.

He shrugged, got my answer from my eyes, and hailed a passing waitress.

If she wasn't on liquor she was on something. Her eyes had a bleak, faraway look. What Charley had said about not expecting too much from her came back to me. I smiled at her but received nothing in return.

"I don't much like this place," she said to me suddenly, as if some conversation were required. She looked around it, giving the room the length and breadth and height of the last scandal she'd heard in it.

I risked a quick glance at Dave and he nodded at me encouragingly.

"Why not?" I asked her.

She shook her head, not sure of her facts. "It's always too cold out here. The food isn't that much." She looked at Dave and then back to me. "Dave said I had to talk to you, Mr. Wright. He said I was supposed to answer your questions. So I will because he's my loving husband." She gave him a quick, venomous look. "Aren't you, sweetie?" She concentrated her attention on me again. I'd seen some people over the years who were on drugs. I thought hers might be some kind of an amphetamine. I bet myself she also had something she took to make her sleep, something she took in the morning to wake her up, something for her nerves, something for her appetite. The result of it all was what I was seeing now. She fumbled in her purse and I was rewarded by the sight of a large pillbox.

"It won't help her any," she said. "I was there that night. I'll be happy to tell you anything you want to know about that monster murdering my brother."

"That's agreeable of you," I said. "Just what exactly did you see her do?"

She gave me a surprised look. "Why, I saw her put

something in his glass," she said quickly. "It was some kind of pill or capsule. I thought it was just something for his poor heart, so I didn't say anything. Then, when Skid was writhing there on the floor, she got that glass away somehow. I never did see how she managed that. She must have given it to that pretty soldier, the one that got killed in Vietnam. The glass was gone and my brother was dead." She leaned forward. "You Wrights are old Lichmont people, aren't you?"

"We were here to greet your family," I said.

She ignored any secondary meaning. "How can you try to help her. This town, your father, before he died, owe us everything. The town would vanish without the plant."

"Maybe," I said. "If the Powell plant weren't here, perhaps there'd be something else."

"No," she said. "It would die without us." She tried to read my eyes with her own, but it was useless. "It's for the money, isn't it. You're trying to get the money for her like Daddy says. It's always the money these days."

"Someone has to help her," I said reasonably. "And a few of the people I talk with seem to think that maybe the Powell family is trying to get her sentenced for something she didn't do. I'm sure you wouldn't want people to continue to say that forever."

"I was there," she said, her voice rising a little. "I know what I saw." I could see people around us trying to listen without appearing to do so. Her husband leaned toward her and tried to capture one of her hands with his, but she avoided him. "You've been talking to that drunken sheriff," she said accusingly to me.

"Easy," he said.

"Shut up," she said contemptuously.

"Mr. Wright's been very nice about all of this," he said to her, his voice a little tougher. "He knows the position we're in at the plant. I'm sure he only wants you to tell him what you saw."

"I'm sorry," she said to me unexpectedly. She nodded and I saw that she wasn't sorry at all.

"You say you saw her take something and put it in Skid's drink?" I asked.

She nodded.

"Where did she take it from?"

"How do you mean?"

"From her purse, a pocket, out of a handkerchief? From where?"

"She took it out of her purse and put it in his drink." She looked away from me, not wanting to see me anymore. "It was some kind of pill, I think."

Hearing Geneva brought back some of the futility of Kate's situation. I nodded as agreeably as I could muster.

"Who else was there close by?"

"Other than my murdered brother?" she asked loudly. "Well, my father and his wife, Susan. David was about somewhere. Charles and one of his sometimes tramps." She nodded maliciously, trying to remember for its effect. "Then some other people from the plant and the town. A couple of soldiers including that one Kate was seeing."

"You mean the one who's dead now, I suppose? The one G.P. had transferred overseas?"

She nodded, not catching it, although Dave Jordan did. He gave me an alarmed look and then subsided.

I smiled at him.

At that moment the door to the terrace opened. G. P. Powell, apparently having dined in baronial splendor, walked through with the careful pace of a man who has drunk very well. He was accompanied by Colonel Uhland and Judge Stickney. I saw G.P. glancing around and I moved so that I would be noticed and stood up by the table. The trio walked purposefully on up to the table.

G.P. said: "I see you're still with us, Mr. Wright. Your questions have made my wife's nerves flare up to the place where she's too ill to be out. I suppose you haven't feelings enough to realize that what you're doing poking around is painful to her." He smiled at me, not really angry.

I nodded. "I suppose you know what you're doing to Kate Powell is more than painful to her and that she's too ill of it to be let out of jail."

He weathered it well, but Judge Stickney, with an audience to perform for, moved forward.

"You, sir, are a jackleg bastard." He eyed me balefully and I grinned at him, knowing that would probably get to him as well as any words.

Colonel Uhland said: "Someone ought to do something about you, Wright." He reached for me with an arm that trembled slightly.

"Not in here, Colonel," G.P. said frostily.

"But maybe last night with a shotgun?" I asked.

The three of them and the Jordans watched me without apparent understanding.

"And maybe someone got bothered about my father, too? Did he bother you, Colonel Uhland?" I nodded at him, watching him closely. "Judge?"

G.P. said: "Your father and I were acquaintances, Mr. Wright. Nothing more, nothing less. I respected him. I'm glad he lost and the state won, but I had nothing against him."

I nodded. "Perhaps. As to whether you've won or not I want you to think about this: Until I'm satisfied that nothing illegal happened at Kate's trial, until I know in my own mind that she poisoned her husband, then I'll be in and about your little town, Mr. Powell. I'll be look-

154

ing and asking questions and trying to find answers. If it takes ten years, I'll be around."

"You won't find anything."

"Oh yes," I said. "I keep finding out things all of the time. Just a while ago I found out that someone in your family managed to put on the pressure to get Captain Joe Ringer transferred. I've found out some of the jury tamperings that went on and expect to find out more about them. I know a lot of things I didn't know yesterday." I nodded at him. "She'll get another trial. If they don't order one at the state level, I'll get her one at the federal level. I don't know whether she committed any crime or not—yet. But I do know that someone put a lot of arm on the trial process." I shook my head. "And all of you are going to find, sooner or later, that you can't do that."

G.P. leaned toward me. "In this town I do what I please, Mr. Wright." He nodded at Geneva and Dave Jordan and turned away. The colonel and Judge Stickney followed. Near the door Charley Powell stood smiling, but G.P., although looking right at him, never saw him.

Dave Jordan said: "Sit down again, Mr. Wright. I want to talk to you a bit more."

Geneva smiled at me. It was a smile that brimmed over with malice.

She said: "Hadn't you better let Mr. Wright get back to whatever it is he's supposed to be doing, dear?" It was a command.

He looked at her for a long moment and then nodded at me. I turned away.

In the morning my mouth tasted of old inner tubes. I've found that no matter how much that stuff costs if you drink very much of eight-year-old this or twelve-year-old that it all turns to skid marks overnight.

We had left the club fairly quickly after G.P. had gone. It was cold on the river and Charley had loaned me his belted trench coat, resplendent with loop and buckles. We'd taken the two girls to Charley's place, a bright steel and chrome apartment with a view of the river and the hills on the far side. Nothing there had been productive and Charley had ended it early.

"Wasn't much of an idea, was it?" he asked.

"Not a bad one," I said.

He nodded. "We'll do it again after things are over here."

I shook my head. "Things will never be over, Charley."

"I should remember that you always were a stubborn man, Mike. But he'll fight you all the way."

"The mere fact that he's the one who's fighting, rather than the state, is extremely suspicious and repugnant to me."

When I was home I locked all of the doors and slept fitfully in Pop's room. But no one came. Except my dream people. They came often enough so that my "bad" leg hurt in the morning. That usually meant a change in the weather. I wasn't sure, right now, that it didn't foretell an impending need for psychiatric help. I was still nervous and jumpy. Maybe that's how I was supposed to be.

I fixed some instant coffee. The bread in the box was moldy and I threw it away.

I drove to the jail after the spartan breakfast. A thin deputy with sorrowful eyes was on duty at the desk. I hadn't seen him before, but he knew me.

"Sheriff said he wanted to see you," he said. "But he went out a while ago and I don't think he'll be back until this afternoon."

"Thank you," I said. "I'll see him later, then. Could I see Kate now?"

156

He got up and got the big key and motioned for me to follow.

"I think she's up," he muttered, more to himself than to me.

The dark hall now smelled of rotting wood, disinfectant, and the morning coffee. He opened a huge iron door. Inside that door there was a little waiting room and beyond that the double barred doors that led to the jail proper. At the side of the waiting room there was another door. Women's quarters. He tapped on the door gently.

"Miss Kate," he said gently to the door. "That lawyer boy's out here and wants to maybe see you." He listened and must have heard something from inside, although I didn't. He turned, winked carefully at me, and left.

I waited.

The door opened a little and I could see her standing in the darkness.

"Come in," she said softly.

I went on into her cell room. It had obviously been equipped for a woman. There was a steel mirror and a tiny dressing table. The toilet cubicle was closed away from the rest of the room by a thin partition. There were a couple of hard chairs and a bed with night table beside it. On the far wall someone had scratched deeply into the plaster: *Jesus Saves*. Someone else had added below: *At Lichmont First Federal*.

I sat down on one of the hard chairs. She hadn't been up very long. She was wearing a bright robe and she'd pulled it tight around her. She wore a kind of fluff thing over her hair. She looked about sixteen years old.

"I'm an awful mess," she said. "I just got up. Alvie and I went over things last night until late. He tried to call you, but there wasn't any answer." Her eyes were inquiring.

"I had to go out last night and check some things," I said. "And you look very lovely."

"Thank you," she said.

She took the other chair and hitched it close to mine. She watched me with eyes I couldn't read and suddenly reached out her hand and touched my face gently. Her hand had a light, perfumed odor.

"I had a dream last night," she said, solemn as a child. She took her hand away and inspected it. "I dreamed it was that summer day I met you." She nodded to herself. "I used to have that dream, but not now for years." She looked up at me. "That day, that time, was something I'd put away."

"We were small children," I said roughly. I shook my head to clear it. There was an aroma in the room, partly jail, partly woman. I was getting excited about the fact we were alone and I knew it wasn't the time to get excited.

"Don't worry about me," she said. "Somehow it's been ruined for me. I don't really care anymore." She stopped, waiting. "Look for me your next life."

"I'll look for you in this one," I said.

She shook her head. "Where are you going?"

"I'm going to drive down to try and see Johnathon Hartwick in Bington. I just wanted to stop past before I went. Don't worry about tomorrow. I'll be with you."

She smiled at me, not really hearing very well what I was telling her, still living in an early-morning fantasy where I was boy and she was girl. She hitched her chair closer so that we were sitting knee to knee.

"Tell me more about Johnathon Hartwick," I said, to hide my nervousness and desire.

"He worked for Skid," she said. "It was a lot more than that, though. They were close. I liked him, too. He was a bumbling man who'd never been able to do anything really right except make people like him. He could mix a good drink and write a bad check, but not much else." She smiled again. "He drank too much. Skid got him out of prison. They were old service buddies." She looked from me for a moment, remembering. "John was a gentle man. He was very big and strong, but not quick up in his head. Not swift. The only time I ever saw him show much emotion was once when he saw Skid hitting me. There was an argument between them. It wasn't that he took sides with me—it was just that he thought Skid shouldn't do that sort of thing. He got Skid drinking with him and shamed him into apologizing." She shrugged. "So I didn't get many lumps from that time on when John was around. When Skid died, John went to pieces. Before he'd always drunk just enough every day to keep going. He was an alcoholic, I guess, but if you didn't look him over carefully you wouldn't know it. I didn't know he was a drunk for a while. After Skid died he lost his ability to control things, to stay on the line. It got too late for him very quickly." She shivered.

"Sometimes it goes like that," I said encouragingly.

"They put him down there after he did some crazy things. He was in jail here for a while. Now they say he hears but doesn't answer. Move his arm or leg and it stays where you move it. They feed him and keep him alive and once I heard that he was getting a little better. Maybe he'll be all right again someday. Maybe never." She moved a little farther toward me, as if to reassure herself that some things were still as she wanted them. "G.P. made him leave the house."

"Did he?"

"Yes. Your father said G.P. had no right to tell him to leave. I was the only one who could do that. But G.P. told him and when John didn't do it, G.P. got some policeman to go out there and arrest John. He was here in jail for part of a day, but they took him on to Bington very quickly. I guess they could see he wasn't acting right and it kept getting worse after they got him admitted at Bington."

"I'll go on down there and see him if they'll let me see him."

"Yes," she said. "If he can understand tell him that I didn't . . ."

"Sure," I said.

I wanted to say something to her about Captain Joe Ringer and maybe ask her about what had happened with Charley, but I decided I wouldn't. It wasn't the time to accuse her. I was supposed to be looking for things to help her.

She got up with me and blocked the door a little with her body, so that I had to squeeze past. I was willing to do that and so I did. She moved more in front of me and took my hand. She gave it a small butterfly kiss. It was a child's thing, rather than the kiss of a woman.

The next one wasn't. Neither were the several thereafter.

I was at the close edge of figuring it was the place and the time when she came up for air and stepped a little away from me.

"I want you," she said so softly that I had to strain to hear it. She shuddered a little. "Not here."

I nodded at her, unable to speak myself. She opened the door for me and sort of pushed me on into the darkness of the hall and on out into the light of the morning beyond the unlocked iron door. I found I was shivering a little in the heat of that morning.

And I wondered just a little if I was now being used by her? It was a cruel thought and one that I put aside. Even if it was true I didn't care a lot. Not enough to admit it to myself.

160

I drove to Bington. Forty miles. I hardly remembered the first thirty.

The mental hospital lay sprawled all over the brow of a large high hill in Bington. No one guarded the outer gate. Inside it there were dozens of ward buildings surrounded by high fencing. Men and women sat on benches in front of the ward buildings and eyed me and my LTD vacantly when I parked in the visitors' area.

The administration building was hushed and quiet. I gave my name and my business at a desk and waited. The receptionist had seen lawyers before and had been instructed about how they should be handled. She had me wait. The only other occupants of the waiting room were a dry-eyed old woman who held tightly to the hand of a wet-eyed young girl. I wondered which was prospective patient. In these days one is never sure.

In a bit a large doctor or attendant dressed all in white came to the door and smiled cheerfully at me.

"Mr. Wright?" he questioned.

I nodded and got up.

"Mr. Hartwick is over in K-11. I'll walk you over there and fill you in a little on the way."

"Thank you."

We went through a set of double doors at the back of the building. The sun was warm on our backs. He helloed other people while I walked silently.

"I don't think he'll say anything," he said apologetically. "Then, again, maybe he will. Some days he mumbles things to me when I take him out in his wheel chair for a walk."

"What kind of things?" I asked.

He shrugged, not trying hard to remember. "I doubt if it would be anything you'd be much interested in."

I shook my head. "I'm interested in about anything. There was a murder. I'm representing a woman who was convicted of killing her husband. Hartwick lived in the same house. He could have done it."

"Sure," he said soothingly. "I'm just a ward attendant. I don't really know much about anything." He shook his head. "He's got this story he keeps repeating over and over. Something about too many drinks and a big party that never gets over." He nodded. "Maybe I can get him started on it for you. It never varies. It's always the same. We'll have to see. Some days nothing will get him to say anything. But I got him to do it for the other man."

"What other man?"

"I forget the name. A big old man. He gave me twenty dollars."

"G. P. Powell?"

He nodded. "I think that was it. He came with a couple of policemen from up there. That was about five days ago."

I nodded. About the time Pop died.

"Thanks for the information."

He nodded and we went on into one of the ward buildings. Down the center hall were dim lights. The hall separated rows of small rooms, all of them locked. I was afraid to look into the tiny, barred windows in the doors, perhaps afraid I might see something very like my own face.

The attendant opened one of the rooms. Inside a huge, doughy man sat in a wheel chair. His face was toward the only wall window, which was barred also. Outside rays of sunlight shone through the trees. He stared at that sunlit window as if it were a television screen, rapt with interest at the show. His eyes kept up the watch when the attendant banged the door closed. The patient had tiny, bright eyes and he looked very old everywhere except those eyes. He was dressed in loose hospital clothing and was clean shaven.

"Someone to see you, Johnathon," the attendant said gently.

The eyes never moved from the window.

The attendant moved up to the chair, caught it by the arms, and heaved it around so that Johnathon's face was to us, the back of his head to the window. The attendant winked at me.

"Tell me about the party, Johnathon," he said softly. "Tell me about the party and all of the drinks and the pretty ladies."

Johnathon's eyes flickered and looked slightly astonished. His mouth opened and the voice that came out was very low and whiny: "There were too many drinks—too many of them. Always too many and so I drank what I could to keep them from him and from the pretty lady. I drank them in the kitchen that night. They had their last party." He stopped. "Then he was gone. Katy, Katy! Too many drinks." A tear came into his right eye and dropped away and then he was crying and the tears ran down his cheeks, but he didn't seem to notice. His head went down and he fell into silence. Then a curious thing took place. As if his eyes knew where the displaced sun was he craned around so that his head turned as far as it could and his body as far as it could without really moving in the chair perceptibly. He could see the sun again, but it must have been painful, if there was pain in the faraway place he now inhabited.

"That's all," the attendant said. "That's all there ever is."

"How long's it been like this?"

"A long time. He was worse when I first got him. I don't know what they call it. He's had a lot of brain damage from heavy drinking. But this is more than that, I suppose. Now he comes up out of it like you saw when you push the right button. Someday maybe he'll come all the way up and out. Or maybe he'll stay like this." He spread his hands.

"Is it possible to see his doctor?"

"He's on vacation. He'll be back next month." He shook his head. "I've heard them talking about Johnathon. Wouldn't do you much good to talk to the doctor, unless you're interested in how he has Johnathon diagnosed. But you can talk to him when he gets back if you want. I guess he's got maybe two hundred patients. Maybe I know more about Johnathon than he does. I feed him and walk him and talk to him when he'll hear me. I take care of him." He laughed without humor. "This is a state institution. The doctor, unless he has the chart in his hand, hardly knows Johnathon's alive." He stopped and studied me. "He said something that had meaning for you, didn't he? Can you tell me what it was?"

"Not anything really," I said.

"All right. I'll make you a deal. You leave me your name and telephone number. If he ever does or says anything else, then I'll get hold of you."

I wrote them down for him on a scrap of paper. On another scrap I took his name and that of Johnathon's doctor.

Before we left the room the attendant gently eased the chair back toward the sunny window so that Johnathon's sun show could go on without permanent muscle damage.

"He can't see the sun. Just the light," he said.

I drove the forty miles back to Lichmont working it through. If I worked on the idea that Kate Powell wasn't guilty, I could theorize about almost everyone, but I really didn't have anything. And yet I felt like I was on the verge of something, as if it was close around me and all I had to do was reach out and touch it. It was a frustrating feeling and failed to improve.

Sheriff Ivan Alvie was waiting for me at the jail. He sat in his leather chair and grinned at me. His eyes were a thousand years old.

"I got you a couple of affidavits from jurors," he said. "Given enough time, I can get more." He shook his head. "Not that it'll do you much good. One of the people I got my affidavit from called a while ago. He said someone else came around after I left. Chief Jett of the Lichmont police department. Chief Jett asked him to sign an affidavit that I'd threatened him to get him to sign my statement. He said he was afraid not to sign and so he signed." He grinned.

"How'd you manage to get the affidavits?" I asked, knowing somehow.

He nodded at me. "I used threats." He thought about it for a minute. "Later, if you want, I can get another affidavit from the juror that Jett got to."

"Did they really pressure the jury, Sheriff? Or am I just getting what you built for me?"

He looked irritated. "It all checked out like I said before. Nothing direct. Nothing heavy-handed. But each juror knew that if he voted innocent that Big Brother Powell would be unhappy and angry. Each juror was made to realize that personally. Judge Stickney helped. He let the jury go home nights. Made it easy to get to them."

A deputy came in and Alvie gave him a pointed look. The man apologized, took something off the desk, and left.

"I told them not to bother in here for a while," he said.

165

"But you can bet that some one of them has already passed the word on to Dave Jordan or G.P. that we're having a war council." He studied me. "How about you, Mike. You seem a little surer of yourself than when I last saw you. Maybe your eyes are more open. Tell me what you found out?"

"Nothing concrete. Doc Bush told me they tried to pressure him and didn't do much good. I found out that G.P. hired a lawyer to go over testimony with the witnesses. That's legal, I guess, but wrong. I discovered the jury foreman is now doing a brisk business with Powell, selling uniforms to them. The Powells had Captain Ringer transferred. But I haven't got anything to convince anyone that Kate didn't kill her husband."

He watched me, oddly satisfied. "You believe her now, though."

I nodded. "I guess I do."

"That's something," he said.

"Won't do us a lot of good once Kate's in prison and maybe awaiting execution. You know and I know that chances are good they'll never execute her no matter what the sentence." I shook my head. "But she expects a miracle from us. She thinks we're going to walk her out of this somehow."

He nodded. "I know."

"I don't have any miracles, Sheriff. Plenty of reasons for an appeal, but no miracles."

He reached in his top desk drawer and came out with a pint bottle of clear liquid. He shook a head on it and set it on the table in front of him. "A miracle," he said without looking at me.

"If that's what I think it hasn't got any help in it for us," I said.

"It's the genuine stuff," he said enthusiastically. "I was

about to offer you a sniff of it. Guaranteed ten days old."

I shook my head and he eyed me regretfully and put the bottle away.

"Tell me what you know about what they're doing out at Powell in the part of the plant that's fenced and guarded?"

"Not much going out there now," he said. "They were fooling with some germ warfare stuff for a time. It got busy as hell, then. Now, they're back down to one shift and the people who work out there say they'll shut it down before too long. The way I hear it they're not making anything out there that they can ship out these days. Nor anything they store. My informants from the plant tell me that all they do out there is control stuff. They go through the motions of manufacturing something, take all the quality control and hazard control precautions they'd take if they were still manufacturing something, but don't actually make anything. Another way for the government to spend our money, I guess."

"When Skid died were they making anything?"

He shook his head. "Not for almost a year. And Skid didn't die from anything out there. Not from what I know about it. I saw what they were making out there once. As far as I know it's all they ever made. And I saw what it could do. A worker got killed. It got hushed up pretty good. They started shutting down right thereafter. He didn't die like they say Skid died. He didn't have fits or muscle twitches or act like a mad dog in the hot sun. And it didn't take him ten or twenty minutes to die. The man out there at the plant just died, quick and sudden."

That shot that theory. It had never been much anyway.

"Died?" I asked.

"One minute he was alive and the next he was dead. What they had out there acts right swift." He looked up at me. "I heard they stopped with it because it was too deadly, too quick. Maybe even those guys up in Washington can get scared."

"That will be the day."

He nodded at me. "Maybe you've seen that day."

I got up. "I'm going over to the office. I want to look over Pop's notes again. I'll be over there for a while if you want me."

"Don't you want to see Kate?"

"Not now." There wasn't anything to say.

I left him there drumming his fingers on his desk. I thought he was thinking about the pint of moonshine, trying to make up his mind.

Outside the wind was hot and the night sky was full of stars. They winked at me, sharing a joke I couldn't understand. There were more of them out there than there were people. Maybe that was part of the joke.

I walked on back to the office. We were down to one light on the steps again. I went on back the dark hall and unlocked. I turned on the overhead fluorescents.

My chair in Pop's office was right in front of the window. Caution made me move into the outer room to the secretary's desk after I'd gotten Kate's file. By the fire escape door.

I dug into it again. I read through the *voir dire* questions and the notes that Pop had taken during the trial, the questions he'd put down to ask of the witnesses, the notes he'd made on the trial testimony to be used in his final argument to the jury.

I didn't see anything. Not anything.

Maybe there was nothing to see.

I went through them again to make sure that there was nothing for me, nothing that came out and hit me with a sledge hammer between the eyes. Nothing that started a prickle up my spine. And couldn't that be it in itself?

I was into it pretty well for the second time when the phone rang.

I picked it up. "This is Alvie," Ivan Alvie said. "Meet me in front of the building. I'll pick you up in ten seconds." His voice was charged with excitement.

"All right," I said to the already silent phone. I locked the door and walked quickly to the stairs. He was already out there. I could see the reflected red from his dome flasher on the steps. He had the car door open and I got in. He stomped away.

"What's up?" I asked over the high whine of the motor.

He looked quickly over at me and shook his head. "I got a call to come out to G.P.'s. Something's happened. I don't know exactly what. I thought I might need a witness in my corner and there you were handy right next door."

"Who called?"

"Mr. Anonymous said something was going on and to get out there," he said. He shook his head again and applied all of his attention to the driving and we wheeled quickly through the jungle of night, the siren and red light scattering sparse traffic ahead of us as a hunter scatters quail.

The lights were on in G.P.'s drive. In front of the house there was an ambulance and a police car. The front door stood wide open. Summer moths fluttered hypnotically around the lights. The sheriff went in at a half run and I followed.

Susan Powell lay on a chaise longue near her pool. Two men in white uniforms were working feverishly over her with respirator apparatus. Someone must have put the Dobermans away. They were not in evidence.

G.P. stood near his wife, wringing his hands anxiously, his back slightly turned to me so that I couldn't see his face. Near him Chief Jett and his driver of the night before, the policeman who'd sought to arrest me, stood talking together. They eyed the sheriff and me with real distaste. I smiled at them.

I moved close to where the men were working over Susan Powell and watched and waited.

One of the men said: "No use, Bill. No use at all. She's been gone for a long while."

The other nodded grudgingly. They moved a wheeled stretcher up and loaded her on. It was hard to recognize her face, dark and constricted in death, but she was wearing the bathing suit I'd seen before.

"What caused it?" I asked.

I was ignored.

I moved carefully on over to where Sheriff Alvie was standing. Chief Jett was giving him information in a biting voice.

"G.P. came home and found her. It's the maid's day off. Mrs. Powell put it in her own coffee, I guess. We won't know for sure until they analyze the contents, but the cup's still there. We think maybe she may have changed her mind after she took it and tried to re-enter the house, but she must have been too far gone to push the sliding doors open. There must have been a lot of it in her coffee. She didn't last very long, I guess."

"A lot of what?" I asked, thinking I knew.

I was ignored again. I was getting used to it by now.

Sheriff Alvie took pity on me. "She wrote a message on top of the beach table over there," he said.

I walked on over and viewed it. Supposedly she had taken what appeared to be lipstick and printed crudely on the table in large, block letters: "I KILLED SKID." An open lipstick tube lay underneath the table.

The message seemed very thoughtful on her part.

It was hard to believe that she would wait this long and then . . .

There was a bottle on the table. It was a plain brown bottle. I got on my knees and, without touching it, I looked carefully into the dark dimness of the bottle. There was a layer of pills or capsules, I wasn't sure of which, in the bottle.

"Strychnine," Chief Jett said from above me. "Or at least we think it's strychnine. G.P. said you'd been out here questioning his wife and got her nervous. Maybe she thought it was all going to be found out and she panicked. Maybe she was remorseful about what she'd done. Or maybe she was just unstable to begin with and kept getting worse."

I got up and looked at him.

"Anyway, it looks like your client is off the hook." He seemed unsatisfied about that. I thought I knew some reasons. Surely there was going to be hell to pay in tomorrow's newspapers. He was going to get a lot of criticism. His police department was going to get more.

I wondered where Susan's death put whatever fight there was for control of Powell Chemicals.

"Where have you been this evening?" Chief Jett asked, maybe reading my mind a little.

I smiled at him. "Ask the sheriff." He didn't really need an answer.

It was hard for something inside me to realize that it was over. Kate Powell would go free.

G.P. said in his belligerent voice: "I still don't believe it. That bitch Kate killed Skid. Susan didn't do it. I don't care about the note. Susan didn't do it. Kate did it." But his voice was halfhearted.

Chief Jett took him aside and talked to him in low, soothing tones. Both men watched me with hate in their eyes.

The sheriff motioned me over.

"Jett called the judge and the prosecutor. The sentencing is off for tomorrow. The judge said to let Kate go on her own recognizance. Jett sort of doubts that Jim True will decide to prosecute her again. So do I." He smiled at me. "Now, do you want to see Kate?"

I managed to smile back. "I do want and need to see her now, Mr. Sheriff."

But all the way back in the car I fought the knowledge of wrongness. Kate had believed in miracles and we'd fallen heir to one. And now she was out, free. What did I care about hunches? I owed this town nothing. But I kept remembering the block letters on the table in red lipstick. I kept remembering they'd said she'd tried to get in the house. I thought of Pop and I saw again, in my mind, the agonized look of asphyxia by poison on Susan's congested face.

I guessed that someone had maybe stood inside that sliding door and held it in place against her frantic scrabbling and coldly watched her die.

I had no use for the town or what it had happily let itself become—a toy for G. P. Powell. But I hated the person who had killed again and again. I couldn't just let it go. Because of Pop. Because of me.

I had a discussion with Sheriff Alvie. He believed, for a while at least, that I needed to go directly back down to Bington and occupy the crazy chair next to Jonathon Hartwick. But only for a while.

I opened the windows a crack in the office. It had been a long time since they were opened. They came up with difficulty, but with the drapes closed and no wind moving down from the north it was about impossible to tell the windows weren't still shut.

Charley came because I'd called him to come. I could hear him on the steps. There was a little pause when he got to where the lone light was, but I could not see any diminution of light in the hall. He was going to be different with me.

I sat in the tiny library, but he could see me from the door. He came in the office and looked all around and seemed satisfied with appearances.

Charley said: "Let's not stay here. Let's go and celebrate somewhere. The club is closed, but my apartment has a rare assortment of good booze for lucky winners."

I smiled at him. "That might be a good idea." I motioned at the file I'd spread on the library table. "Just trying to get everything straightened around in my mind. So there aren't any loose ends."

He looked past me at the fire escape door. I thought his eyes were sharp enough to pick up the hint of deeper blue where the nail had been wedged to hold the door. He nodded at the blue and at me.

I shook my head at him and at the file. "When I got to looking things over and thinking about what had happened the night Skid was poisoned, it seemed to me to be an impossible situation. Here's a man sitting in the midst of a party of sorts and everyone there could have poisoned him."

"Good thing it was Susan," he said.

"I never gave her much consideration before. She might have wanted to poison her husband, but I couldn't see any reason she'd poison Skid. And Skid drank bourbon and

173

cola while G.P. is a bourbon and water man. Little chance of getting those mixed up. I talked to her once at the house before G.P. interrupted us. I thought Susan was telling me the truth. I was pretty sure that she'd tell anyone the truth. Anne Silver, Pop's secretary, thought so too."

"I hear she left a confession. And they say she committed suicide," Charley said. "That's damned good evidence you're wrong, my boy."

"Maybe I'm just stupid," I admitted. "But it kind of goes back to my father, seems to me. He was always a meticulous man. Yet he seemed to have fumbled Kate's trial a little. His notes looked a little to me as if he'd kept right at it up to a certain point, then just sort of eased off. Jim True, an old, honored opponent, said something about it. Kate thought he might have been sick." I looked up at him. "You helped him a little. Did you notice anything, Charley?"

"Not me," he said, face mystified.

"I guess he could maybe have found out the information on your family that you gave him in some other places?"

He nodded. "I suppose."

"I kept forgetting to ask you and I never did find out from you—was strychnine available in the part of Powell where the military is located? I mean, so that Captain Ringer could have easily furnished it to Kate?"

He looked crestfallen. "I forgot to ask."

"And they told me you called the police, Charley. I wanted to ask why you did that. When Skid died?"

"He was dead. One normally calls them."

"Maybe you'd call an ambulance. A doctor was there. You didn't need a doctor. But why the police?"

He eyed me carefully. "He was having these spasms all over the floor. I knew something was wrong. Someone said to call the police. I guess I called them plus an ambulance. I don't really remember now. If you say I did call them, then I guess I did."

"Okay," I said amiably. "After they found Susan I talked to Kate about her stock. I guess she'll be able to vote it now. The temporary injunction was only good for ninety days and will run out before the meeting." I looked up at him. "Her stock can make the difference, can't it?"

He gave me his finest smile. "You know it can, Mike. I told you that. With Kate voting it for me I'm pretty near a cinch." He nodded at me, pleased. "I'm glad you called me, very glad it all worked out so well. And I want you to know that what benefits me can and will benefit you. I promise it to you. Forget politics. Stay here. I'll pay you more money than you can make in a million political years. I'll give you an option on some stock so you can have a piece of the action. You can take over my old job, but it'll be a new job now, a working job. We'll make things hum out there."

"Sure," I said. "But help me a little while longer, Charley. I'm still straightening things out in my head. Like I said, anyone could have killed Skid."

He moved a little closer to me. His eyes seemed wary now. My reaction hadn't been what he expected. "Let's talk the whole thing over later. I've got the Continental parked outside. We can buzz somewhere."

"Not yet," I said. "Did you tell my father you had someone on the jury who would tie it up, make it hang?"

He shook his head.

"That's strange. It would explain a lot of things. Pop had circled a juror's name. It seemed like he let up a little in the trial, wasn't as meticulous as usual. If you'd told him that you had a juror in your pocket I could maybe figure why. Why he didn't venue it out of the county?" I shook my head, thinking.

"He might have believed that, but I never promised it," Charley said.

I nodded, dismissing it for the minute. "Then Pop went out to G. P. Powell's after the trial. G.P. said he didn't talk to him. I figured maybe he was talking to Susan. She didn't say, but I didn't ask. Pop probably didn't learn much, but if someone was watching, it was a good sign he wasn't going to let things alone."

"You're very like him in that way," Charley said.

"Thank you. And then I found that no one at Powell goes from the Army reservation part to the factory part. There are tough guards, dogs and fences. I found out Kate never visited either part of the plant. It would have been difficult for her or her supposed lover to obtain strychnine. Difficult, but not impossible. It's fairly easy to get hold of. But to just poison someone the thing that they were working with for the Army was far superior."

"Susan solved the problem," he said confidently.

"Not exactly." I looked up at him again and waited until he was looking back at me. "You see, my father called me the night he died. I haven't told anyone about that yet. He told me first that 'he'd been jabbed good.' He didn't say 'we,' but 'he.' He told me some other things, but they can wait for now. Let's get to Miss Susan again. Here, outside the pool, are her beautiful, dangerous Dobermans. They didn't attack anyone the night she was killed. Maybe they weren't even there. I didn't ask. I'll ask later. Maybe they were there and didn't attack whoever it was because they knew that person. Or maybe that person was inside the house when the poison began to take effect, holding the door so that Susan and/or her Dobermans couldn't get into the house. If someone had poisoned her then that poisoner would want to stay and make sure nothing went wrong."

"G.P., then," he said, giving Susan up for the moment.

"Why? Skid was his favorite son. They got along well. Skid running the plant was like G.P. running it. If Skid died, then G.P. probably would have known that he *could* lose control. I'm sure he knew the contents of Skid's will. Why would he water the situation? He's a mean old bastard, but I never pictured him killing Skid. And I found his anger against Kate, although it was misdirected, seemed genuine. He took all of the steps he could against Kate and your scared little town out there let him take them. When Susan died he was still on the same idea—Kate had done it. He didn't want to believe otherwise."

"Maybe it could have been Johnathon Hartwick," he said. "I remember in law school when someone once lectured to us about polygraphs. They make mistakes on those things and Johnathon did wind up in a nut house after Skid died. Maybe he was crazy at the time and his being crazy affected the polygraph tests." He nodded at me.

"I went down to see him earlier today at Bington. I'm convinced he's spent his whole life in one gigantic party. When Skid died the party was over for him. Now it's the morning after. There's a long hangover ahead. Maybe he'll never come out of it. Maybe he will. All I found out was that he's a mental case. Let's say that I'm willing to accept the polygraph that cleared him. So Johnathon's out for my purposes now."

"How come Kate flunked, then?"

"She didn't flunk," I said. "They just didn't get a good run on her. That happens. Or maybe G.P. paid someone off. He paid off a lot of people. Just let me wander on for a moment. You might find it interesting. It had to be someone who'd thought about it, planned it for a while, and who benefited by it someway."

He shook his head. "I can't believe that Geneva or Dave would do anything to Skid." He gave me a look full of malice. "Not that Dave didn't move up in the world, to the place I ought to be, when Skid was killed. Geneva liked that. And she'd know about pills."

"No," I said. "Geneva lives in a world where she will always be unwell. She lives on her speed pills and her tranquillizers. I couldn't find or hear of anything about her relationship with Skid that wasn't friendly. And when Skid died she couldn't benefit from his death. Unless it was very indirectly." I nodded at him and saw that his eyes were in shadow and that he had something in his coat pocket that he was nervously caressing. I couldn't see the outline of it, but it seemed heavy. "Same thing applies to her husband. He was outside with the colonel when Skid died. Bad alibi, but good enough for me. Unless both Dave and the colonel were liars. Possible, but not probable." I smiled at him. "But you went to Kate's aid, didn't you, Charley?"

He nodded. "And I'm proud of it now. Your father was right, I was right, you're right."

"And the town was wrong." I watched him carefully. "Like I said, you helped Pop with the trial. You fed him information. In a town where Powell people were bound to be on the jury you made the recommendations. And I think you picked those people who you knew were most susceptible to pressure. Maybe you even secretly helped put some of the pressure on them. All a part of the scheme, wasn't it, Charley? You were going to take control at the plant. You were going to grab it no matter what was in the way. You hate your father. Both of us know that. And I remember you from law school. You're a competitor. You

178

want to win *now*, not at some time in the future. You want to win at this meeting." I nodded. "Then, if you did win, if it did go your way, you were sure you could cover up whatever needs covering without trouble. The tame town policemen could change their leader when you won." I thought for a moment. "I'll bet if I dig back far enough that I'll find you're the one who was the Powell troop leader in the war against the election of Sheriff Ivan Alvie. You couldn't control him. He could hurt your plan so you badmouthed him to G.P. and the rest and tried to elect someone else." I nodded again and something in his eyes made me think I was right.

I lied: "I have a witness who saw a man in uniform outside Skid's house when the sirens were sounding and Skid was beating his life out against the floor. Just a casual observer I stumbled over. He saw a man with a pretty woman. Maybe he can still identify that man, maybe not. He'll get a chance now. It could have been you in that fancy trench coat you let me wear on the river. That could be the 'uniform.' You got Skid's glass. It would have been possible for you in all the excitement. Just switch glasses. You took his glass out into the yard as if it was your drink. You had a woman with you, either a date or someone from the party. You dropped the glass in the yard. Accidentally, it seemed. That gave you an excuse to have the glass washed. It had dirt on it. But it was cold and people don't normally wash glasses in that kind of weather. I figure you did it to confuse things. Kate's prints were on the glass. Yours were also. You couldn't wear gloves at the party. And so the glass had to disappear."

He shook his head idly, his eyes still in shadow. I moved a little closer to the fire escape door and he smiled thinly at me.

"You say I did all of this. But why? I didn't profit when

Skid died. Kate profited. So did Geneva and G.P. But not me."

I nodded. "Not moneywise. But you knew your father well enough to know that he would block Kate from voting her shares when Skid died. Even if he didn't block her you didn't think, under existing circumstances, she'd vote them for you. But now she can vote them. Things have changed. You are preferable to G.P. She'll vote them for you. The injunction isn't worth anything now. Half of Skid's shares. All you had to do for them was to convict her and then, right at the final moment, right when you knew the scandal would hurt the management of the plant worst, unconvict her. So you saved the poison. And you went out to see your father's wife, Susan. You put some in her strong black coffee. She liked coffee. I saw her drinking it at the house that day. She drank it. You let her thresh her life away. To make sure she couldn't get aid, call anyone, you held the door on her and you waited there until she was pretty nearly gone."

"You're tiresome," he said. "This mess is done with. You've got what you wanted. You haven't got anything else."

I nodded. "Oh yes. I've got several things. My witness isn't much, I'll admit. I doubt he can identify you, but I want you to know one thing for certain, one thing about which I'll testify."

He shrugged. "I know you're going to tell me, so why should I fight it?"

"Like I said, Pop called me that night, Charley. He wanted me to set up a meet with the governor for him."

"The governor's not really going to help you in this," he said. "You fooled the others, but not me. I called him. I got him to promise to leave it alone. You're on your own."

He smiled. "It's amazing what the promise of a large donation can do."

"Okay," I said. "So the governor won't help. But check the phone company. There'll be a record. Pop did call me. And he told me about his suspicions." The last was an outright lie again, but it made him blink. I followed it up: "He said you'd set him up. You made him think it was all fixed —that you had someone on the jury who'd hang it for him and then he could get bond for Kate. He told me that. That's why I came down and stayed." I nodded at him. "That's why I've been watching you. I know, Charley. And when Kate knows she'll *never vote those stocks your way*. You'll sit in some air-conditioned Florida bar for the rest of your life. Thirty-six holes a day for you, Charley. Useless."

He smiled. "But Kate doesn't know yet, does she?"

"No," I said. "Not yet. She will soon."

He did have a gun in his pocket. He took it out and pointed it at me. I was impressed by it.

"I didn't need one for your father," he said. "I just waited up there at the head of the stairs and whacked him with a piece of pipe when he came past. Then I pushed him on down. But you're bigger and younger. I brought this along to make sure. I'm going to put you in my car and take you to your father's house."

"Where you shot at me with the shotgun?" I asked.

He shook his head. "Not me," he said.

"Oh," I said, not believing him.

"I'll take a stick and write you a farewell note in the dirt. Your work is done. You're despondent about your father. You never had a wife. He was the last thing you had left. So you're going to kill yourself. Maybe you can sit in that relic Buick of his and turn on the motor and die from monoxide. Our local police will be anxious to believe it. Maybe we'll just look around and decide." He reached in the other pocket. "I've got some pills here. You can take them and it'll be easy for you."

"The sheriff will never believe it."

He nodded. "He will if I'm running Powell, and I will be. No one cares about you, Mike. You and your father were nothings. You got in my way."

"Why strychnine for Skid, Charley?" I asked. "There are lots of poisons around that are quicker and surer."

"Poisons that a man with a degree in pharmacy would know about and a citizen might not. I can name a hundred, but I wanted something simple for both of them."

"Then you did plan them together?"

He nodded. "Sure. Like you said. It's my plant. I should run it. Things and people got in my way. So I removed them. I'm sorry about your dad. He had a tough case. I brought him a gift. He should have looked better into it." He grinned. "He was pretty surprised when that jury came back."

"He had a juror's name circled. The guy who was foreman. Was he supposed to be the one?"

"I never told him which one. The circle would be a guess. I just told him I had one and to take it easy on the *voir dire*. So he did and we wound up with a tough jury. I told him I was as shocked as he was. But I knew he wasn't going to let it alone. He started looking at me like you are now. So I had to take care of him." He shook his head. "I didn't know he'd called you, though. I'm still not sure that's the truth. But I wanted you to come down. Someone had to be here for her to get things turned around. You were admirable."

I said: "And Miss Susan?"

"She was just the logical one." He shook his head. "I had no problems with her. I put it in her coffee. A lot of it.

She got up to the door and was beating on it. I had it pulled tight. The dogs were inside the garage. They wouldn't have bothered me anyway, so I never even thought of them. When she started another spasm I didn't want her found right there in front of the door. So I carried her back out and to the chaise and wrote her final message. I was fairly sure she was gone but I was going to wait until I was positive. I thought I heard a car. I'd parked away from the house. So I went out the front. There wasn't anyone there yet. I hadn't gotten her prints on the bottle." He shook his head, disgusted. "I watched until G.P. came and then I called your friend, the sheriff. They won't print the bottle, anyhow. Not with her confession."

I moved closer to the door. I could touch the handle now by just extending my hand.

"Won't do you any good," he said. "I jammed it one day when I was up here. The last day of Kate's trial. I wanted to make sure your father couldn't get out that way."

"Sure," I said. "It *had* to be someone who could get in or out of his office. Another reason you were the only logical one."

"It's still jammed." He waved the gun. "Come on now."

I slowly reached out my hand and flung the door wide open.

All that I saw in his eyes was an enormous look of surprise.

"I took your nail out and colored a match in some ink," I said. "Made it look about the same."

Outside on the rickety fire escape landing three men stood. G. P. Powell, Jim True, and Sheriff Ivan Alvie. Alvie had a gun pointed directly at Charley's midsection. Charley let his own drop to the floor.

I wanted very badly to hurt him and I thought I knew a way. "I had Sheriff Alvie bring G.P. I thought the two of you might have great fun trying to compete for the buying price on jurors when your trial comes up. You're his son all right, Charley. Just like him."

He gave us all that very best smile. Maybe something he'd learned in law school made him say nothing else. He stood there smiling and Sheriff Alvie handcuffed him while G.P. watched, his face cold and hard, hating all of us.

I went out past the house before I picked up Kate. Out in the garage I got a bucket of paint and a thin brush. I drove down to City Hall. It was in the early hours of the morning. The sidewalk was cool and the sun was not due for some hours. No one seemed to be watching me. There was enough light reflected from inside the police station so that I could see. No one came out. I opened up the paint and refurbished the obscene sign some hippie or vandal or rebel had painted in front of the hall, not really caring much whether I was seen or not. When the sign was finished I felt childishly satisfied.

It seemed to me that the breeze was coming up a little when I was done and parts of the night stars were covered.

The town's record was complete. My witnesses, the ones who'd seen the police roust me on the riverbank, had never appeared. Someone must have paid or threatened them away. Even the governor had sold me out. Lichmont and its police had been so busy trying to get a possible piece of the money or at least placate the money that no one had bothered to look further than the inside of his/her pocketbook.

And I still didn't know whether Kate would have gotten the house whether she'd stayed convicted or not.

I got in the car and started it and had to pull over and stop it to laugh at myself halfway to the sheriff's office. Something told me that the sheriff had shotgunned my room, making sure the pellets went high over me. It had to be that way. I hadn't been dead serious enough for him and so he'd made me a little more receptive to the town around me.

G.P. would have had his people aim a mite lower.

I picked Kate up at the jail. Maybe someday I'd ask the sheriff about that shotgunning, but tonight I just shook his hand and left him smiling as we drove away. Kate had only one thin suitcase of her possessions. I wondered if all of the money would bother me and thought it might.

She held my hand and I drove carefully with the one that was left, aware that the governor's traffic safety committee wouldn't care much for that sort of driving conduct.

She watched me as if I was the end of the world.

I could always practice law. If they didn't like me up there, if they'd really sold me out, as I thought they probably had, then I'd forget politics. I thought I'd have to forget, but I was going to make them help me say it.

At the outskirts of town a thin rain began to fall. I drove north, with Kate smiling there beside me.